LONE STAR COUNTRY CLUB
EST. 1923

*Where Texas society reigns supreme—
and appearances are everything.*

CAST OF CHARACTERS

Phillip Westin joined the Lone Star Country Club to meet nice girls and to forget about the not-so-nice one who broke his heart years ago. But when his ex comes to town, trouble isn't far behind. To keep her safe, Westin must rely on his tough-guy instincts to discern truth from lie, and his friends from his enemies.

Celeste Cavanaugh, aka Stella Lamour, can't remember a time when she didn't have stars in her eyes. These days, though, the stars are pretty tarnished, and a happily-ever-after in the sizzling embrace of her personal hero, Phillip Westin, doesn't sound so bad.

Cole Yardley had only met Celeste once, but he'd remember her anywhere. When the shadowy ATF agent comes to town to investigate a gun-smuggling ring in quiet little Mission Creek, Texas, he threatens to blow Celeste's secrets and her chances with Phillip away.

Dear Reader,

Top off your summer reading list with six brand-new steamy romances from Silhouette Desire!

Reader favorite Ann Major brings the glamorous LONE STAR COUNTRY CLUB miniseries into Desire with *Shameless* (#1513). This rancher's reunion romance is the first of three titles set in Mission Creek, Texas—where society reigns supreme and appearances are everything. Next, our exciting yearlong series DYNASTIES: THE BARONES continues with *Beauty & the Blue Angel* (#1514) by Maureen Child, in which a dashing naval hero goes overboard for a struggling mom-to-be.

Princess in His Bed (#1515) by *USA TODAY* bestselling author Leanne Banks is the third Desire title in her popular miniseries THE ROYAL DUMONTS. Enjoy the fun as a tough Wyoming rancher loses his heart to a spirited royal-in-disguise. Next, a brooding horseman shows a beautiful rancher the ropes…of desire in *The Gentrys: Abby* (#1516) by Linda Conrad.

In the latest BABY BANK title, *Marooned with a Millionaire* (#1517) by Kristi Gold, passion ignites between a powerful hotel magnate and the pregnant balloonist stranded on his yacht. And a millionaire M.D. brings out the temptress in his tough-girl bodyguard in *Sleeping with the Playboy* (#1518) by veteran Harlequin Historicals and debut Desire author Julianne MacLean.

Get your summer off to a sizzling start with six new passionate, powerful and provocative love stories from Silhouette Desire.

Enjoy!

Melissa Jeglinski
Senior Editor, Silhouette Desire

Please address questions and book requests to:
Silhouette Reader Service
U.S.: 3010 Walden Ave., P.O. Box 1325, Buffalo, NY 14269
Canadian: P.O. Box 609, Fort Erie, Ont. L2A 5X3

ANN MAJOR

Shameless

Silhouette®

Desire

Published by Silhouette Books

America's Publisher of Contemporary Romance

Special thanks and acknowledgment are given to Ann Major for her contribution to the LONE STAR COUNTRY CLUB series.

This book is dedicated to Ella Mae Lescuer for all her hard work.

 SILHOUETTE BOOKS

ISBN 0-373-76513-4

SHAMELESS

Books by Ann Major

ANN MAJOR

lives in Texas with her husband of many years and is the mother of three grown children. She has a master's degree from Texas A&M at Kingsville, Texas, and is a former English teacher. She is a founding board member of the RWA and a frequent speaker at writers' groups.

Ann loves to write; she considers her ability to do so a gift. Her hobbies include hiking in the mountains, sailing, ocean kayaking, traveling and playing the piano. But most of all she enjoys her family.

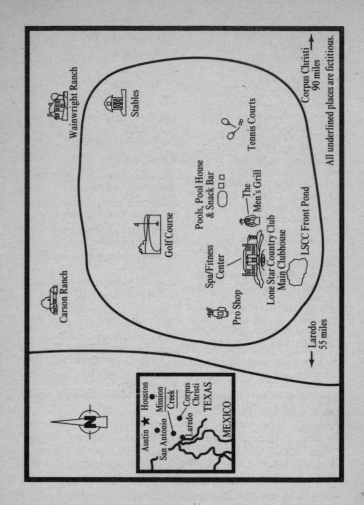

Carson Ranch

Wainwright Ranch

Stables

Golf Course

Pools, Pool House & Snack Bar

Tennis Courts

Spa/Fitness Center

Pro Shop

The Men's Grill

Lone Star Country Club Main Clubhouse

LSCC Front Pond

Laredo 55 miles

Corpus Christi 90 miles

All underlined places are fictitious.

Austin ★

Houston

Mission Creek

San Antonio

Corpus Christi

Laredo

TEXAS

MEXICO

N

Prologue

Lt. Col. Phillip Westin, burly ex-Marine, wasn't dead.

Hell. He almost wished he was. Solitary confinement—it made you crazy.

Groggily, he chafed at the ropes binding his wrists and ankles. Beneath the restraints his skin burned from too much rubbing.

He tried to roll over but he was so weak he could only lie facedown in the dark, gasping. The windowless walls seemed to close in upon him. He wanted to scream…or worse…to weep. One minute he was burning up, the next he was shivering and whimpering on his cot like a baby. The cramps in his legs and arms knifed through him constantly.

Where the hell was he? *Remember! Try to remember.* His thoughts were slow and tortured. It took him a while to realize that he was lying on a dirty canvas cot deep in The Cave that served as the dungeon underneath *Fortaleza de la Fortuna.* The *fortaleza* was a terrorist compound in Mezcaya run by a particularly dangerous group of thugs who went by the name El Jefe.

Westin had been captured a few weeks ago shortly after he'd run Jose Mendoza, one of the terrorist ringleaders, off a mountain road and killed him. Too bad Mendoza's illegitimate son, Xavier Gonzalez, didn't have a forgiving nature.

Westin blinked but couldn't see a thing. The damned dungeon was blacker than the inside of an ape's behind.

His head throbbed where Xavier had smacked him with a rifle butt yesterday. His throat was dry. He was thirsty as hell. Dehydrated probably.

Xavier and his unkempt dirty bunch of thugs had captured him and beaten him senseless and then gleefully trussed him like a pig for slaughter.

He was going to die. At dawn. A single bullet to the head, the final coup de grace. An hour ago Xavier and a couple of short, teenage captors reeking of body odor had strutted inside The Cave like a bunch of bantam cocks in a barnyard and kicked him with their black, muddy combat boots.

"Gringo. ¿Cómo estás?" They'd prodded him with their assault rifles and made cruel jokes in Spanish rather than in their Mezcayan dialect. They'd flipped coins to see who'd get lucky enough to pull the trigger. Xavier, the youngest and the most lethally handsome, had slid a .45 out of a black holster and dried it off on his sleeve.

"You kill my father, so you die, *gringo.* You have no right to be in my country."

"Your drug and gun money was making inroads in *my* town, *bastardo*. *My* town."

The kid was dark with a permanent Mezcayan tan. With one brown hand he'd lifted a cigarette to his pretty mouth; with the other he'd carefully centered the cold barrel on Phillip's forehead.

"*Your* town?"

Xavier's eyes were scarily irrational in his pretty-boy face. His finger had pulled back the trigger ever so slightly. "Bang. Bang, *gringo. Your* town is going to be my town."

Before Phillip could argue, the thick, acrid cigarette smoke from the kid's cigarette had made him wretch. Hell, maybe puking up his guts had saved him. Instead of firing his gun, Xavier had burst out into hysterical laughter and shrieked, "*Cobarde*. Coward."

Then the *bastardo* had danced a little jig.

"*Tengo sed*. I'm thirsty," Phillip had said.

Xavier had smiled that pretty smile. "So—drink this!" He'd pitched the cigarette into the vomit in front of Phillip's face.

Bastardos. His death was a game to them. Phillip Westin, ex-Marine, had been handpicked for the Alpha Force. His usual style was spit-and-polish perfect.

He wouldn't be a pretty corpse. He wouldn't even rate a body bag in this hellhole compound that was hidden deep in Mezcayan mountains and rain forest.

There'd be no military honors at his funeral. No funeral, period. No beautiful woman to weep over his grave back home in south Texas.

Suddenly a blond goddess, no a witch, seemed to float above him in the misty black.

Oh, God…. Just when he was weak, wet, shaking and puking with fear, he had to think of *her*—the icy, trampy witch, who'd walked out on him. Usually, the witch was satisfied to haunt his dreams. When he was awake, he was disciplined enough to keep his demons and witches at bay.

But he was weak and cold…so cold and feverish a spasm shook him…and so scared about dying he could think only of her.

Anger slammed him when her sulky, smoky voice began to sing the love song she'd written about their doomed relationship.

He jerked at his ropes, and to his surprise they loosened just a bit. "Go away! Leave me alone!" he yelled into the steamy darkness.

The perverse phantom draped her curvy body against the black wall and sang louder.

Nobody but you/Only you.

"Shut up," he growled even as every cell in his body began to quiver as he fisted and unfisted his fingers in an attempt to free his hands.

I had to say goodbye…but everywhere I go…there's nobody in my heart…only you….

Her husky voice had his head pounding. He dug his fingernails into his palms. Suddenly to his surprise, he jerked his right hand free of the ropes. "Damn you, shut the hell up!"

And yet I had to say goodbye, the witch crooned.

"Tramp! You're just a one-hit wonder. You know that, don't you?"

That shut her up, but she didn't go away. Instead, that sad, vulnerable expression that could tie him in knots came into her eyes, which shone brilliantly in the dark. Her golden hair fell in silken coils around her slim shoulders.

Hell. She looked like a little lost sex kitten in need of a home and a warm bed. His home. His bed.

Oh, God, all she ever had to do was look at him like that and all he wanted to do was to hold her and to protect her and to make love to her. What would he give to have her one more time before he died?

Everything—

His gut cramped as he clawed his cot with his free hands. He remembered exactly how her hair smelled, how her skin smelled, how her blue eyes flashed with tears if he got too domineering. She'd had a fearsome talent for gentling him.

Escape. He had to escape.

His hands shook. He closed his eyes and tried not to remember how small she was or how perfectly she'd fit him.

Think of something else! Like getting out of here!

But when he swallowed, he tasted her. One taste, and he was as hard as a brick.

Somehow he got the ropes around his ankles loose, but when he tried to stand, the black walls spun and he fell back onto the cot. Weak as he was, his groin pulsed with desire. Hell. The proximity of death was the best aphrodisiac.

Damn Celeste Cavanaugh. He'd asked her to be his wife, to marry him. What a damn fool he'd been to do that. Hell, he'd picked her up in a bar. No. Damn it. He'd rescued her from a bar brawl. She'd been a nobody from the gutter, the prettiest, sexiest little nobody in the whole world with a voice like an angel.

He'd lifted her out of that life, given her everything, and treated her like a lady. She'd moved in with him and they'd played at love and marriage. Why the hell hadn't she bothered to tell him about her ridiculous ambition to be a country-western star? Why hadn't she at least given him a chance to understand it?

As soon as she'd gotten on her feet, she'd run to Vegas with another man. Phillip had come home from a dangerous mission in the Middle East where he'd gone to rescue his buddies. His homecoming had been delayed because he'd been captured and had had a narrow escape. But once home again, he'd thrown his seabag down at the door, stalked through the ranch house, calling her name. God, all those days and nights when he'd been a hostage trapped in that cell in the Middle East, he'd been burning up for her. Just like now.

She'd left him a letter on his pillow.

"I met a man, who's going to get me an audition with a world-famous producer, Larry Martin. I'll call you from Vegas." She'd said her stage name was Stella Lamour.

There had been more letters in the mailbox from Stella. After he'd read and reread those letters, every word carving his heart out, something had died inside him. Maybe his feelings.

Forget her.

But he couldn't. Seven years later, she still starred in all his dreams.

When he died down here, she wouldn't even know. The *bastardos* would sling his bloody corpse into the jungle, and he'd rot. In this rain and heat and mud, he'd be fertilizer in less than a month.

You're an ex-Marine. Forget her.

When he tried to stand again, he passed out and dreamed he was back home in Texas dancing with her at the Lone Star Country Club while his Marine buddies cheered and clapped.

He regained consciousness to heat that was as thick and dark as a sauna, to no-see-ums eating him alive. To explosions and heavy boots stomping down some corridor.

Dawn. Time to die.

Was there a weepy, pink light sifting through the single crack in the ceiling or was he hallucinating again?

Shouts in Spanish were followed by more heavy footsteps. Then the lock on the heavy door clicked. The door banged. Flashlights danced in the dark, blinding him.

''Xavier?'' Westin squinted. Terror gripped him like a fist. He felt so weak and vulnerable he muttered a quick prayer.

Cobarde. Xavier's contempt still stung.

In those last fleeting seconds before certain death, Phillip's life flashed in front of him in neon color—his lonely childhood in his mother's Houston mansion with all those rooms that echoed as a solitary little boy walked through them in search of love.

Nobody had ever wanted him…until Patricia, his college sweetheart. For a time she'd seemed so perfect, but in the end, she hadn't wanted him enough to understand his determination to see the world and become a Marine.

Neither had Celeste. Both his loves had left him.

The flashlight zeroed in on his face, blinding him again. What was the use? He held up his hands in surrender. All he said was, ''If you're going to kill me, just be done with it.''

Cobarde.

''Not tonight, sir,'' said a familiar respectful voice that slammed Westin back to his days in the Marines, back to the Gulf War. Phillip's eyelids stung when he tried to stand. Once again his legs crumpled beneath his weight. The lights spun and he nearly fainted.

''Friends,'' came that familiar, husky voice that made Phillip's eyes go even hotter.

"Tyler…."

Westin blinked. Ty Murdoch, his handsome face painted black and green, his night-vision glasses dangling against his broad chest, towered above him like a warrior god.

"Tyler—"

Phillip was trying to stand but was falling again when Tyler's strong arms grabbed him and slung him over his broad back in a fireman's lift.

"You're going home," a woman said.

"Celeste?"

Before the beautiful woman could answer, Phillip fainted.

He was going home. Home to Celeste.

When he opened his eyes, they were beyond the compound, hunkering low in the tangle of bushes on the edge of the lavish lawns. Dimly he was aware of the pretty woman cradling his head in her lap.

"Celeste?"

He was sweating and freezing at the same time.

An eternity later he looked up and saw a chopper coming in hot, kicking up dust and gravel before settling on the ground.

A rock that felt like a piece of hot metal gouged Phillip's cheek.

"Damn."

Then Ty was back lifting him, up…up…into the chopper. They took off in a hurry. They were going home.

Home to Celeste.

He shut his eyes and saw Celeste…blond and pretty, her eyes as blue as a Texas sky. She was crying, her

cheeks glistening. The image, even if it was false, was
better than a funeral.

Phillip's hand shook as he lifted the razor. He paused,
staring at the gaunt face with the slash across the cheek.
It had been seven days since the rescue, and he was still
as weak as a baby.

When the infirmary door slammed open, he jumped
like a scared girl, panicking at the sound of boots because they reminded him of Xavier. The razor fell into
the sink with a clatter.

In the mirror, the dark-haired stranger with the hol-
lowed-out silver eyes was pathetic. By comparison the
darkly handsome man who strode up behind him was
disgustingly robust.

"Mercado?"

Ricky flashed his daredevil grin. "Good to see you
up and about."

"Yeah." Westin had to grip the sink with tight fingers
so he wouldn't fall. No way was he walking back to the
hospital bed. No way would he let Mercado gloat at how
wobbly he was.

"After this, you'd better lay low, *amigo*. You stirred
up a hornet's nest."

"You think I don't know that."

"El Jefe's big. And not just down here. They're well
connected in Texas."

"Why the hell do you think I came down—"

"These guys won't give up. They'll be gunning for
you and yours."

"There is no yours. She left me, remember." Phillip
shut up. He didn't want to talk about *her*. Still, Mercado
was one of the few who knew about Celeste. Most of
his buddies believed he'd never gotten over his first love,

Patricia, the classy girl he'd loved in college—the proper girl. It was better that way, better not to cry on their shoulders about a trashy singer he'd picked up in a bar and been stupid enough to fall for.

"Yeah, and Celeste's the reason you've had a death wish for seven damn years."

"Shut up."

"You're forty-one, *amigo.*"

"You make that sound old."

"Too old for this line of work."

"This was personal. You know that. The bastards were moving into Mission Creek. They were using kids to run guns. Kids—"

"Why don't you go back to your ranch? Find a nice, churchgoing girl, get married and hatch some rug rats."

"Sounds like fun. What about you? You straight? Or are you gonna run arms for the family? What the hell were you doing down there?"

Mercado scowled. "Saving your ass."

"You had some help."

"What does it take? A declaration written in blood. Like I told you—I'm straight."

"You'd better be."

His face and eyes dark with pain, Mercado shut up and stared at the floor. Phillip felt instant remorse. "Ty told me you were useful in the Mezcaya rescue," Phillip admitted.

"I'm surprised he said—"

"He did. Thanks. I owe you…for what you did for Ty. And for me."

Suddenly Westin was no longer in the mood to question the character of a man who'd helped save him. The heated exchange had left him so weak, Mercado's dark face began to swirl. His fingers couldn't seem to hold on to the sink. No way could he shave.

"Oh, God," he muttered as the gray tiles rushed up to meet him.

Mercado lunged, barely catching him before he fell.

"Find that nice girl," Mercado muttered. "Lean on my arm, old buddy, and we'll get you back to bed."

"Hell. I don't go for nice girls. I like 'em hot...and shameless."

"Maybe it's time for a change of pace...in your old age."

"Old age?" Stung, Phillip almost howled. The truth was, a ninety-year-old was stronger than he was. Oh, God, why was it such a damn struggle to put one foot in front of the other? When he finally made it to the bed, he was gasping for every breath. He let go of Mercado and fell backward.

His head slammed into the pillow. Even so, they both managed a weak laugh.

"Get the hell out of here, Mercado."

"Forget shameless. Find that churchgoing girl, old man."

Mercado waved jauntily and saluted. Then the door banged behind him and he was gone.

One

Stella Lamour grabbed her guitar and glided out of the storeroom Harry let her use as a dressing room. After all, a star had to have a dressing room. She tried to ignore the fact that the closet was stacked with cases of beer, cocktail napkins and glasses...and that the boxy, airless room gave her claustrophobia when she shut the door.

Some dressing room.... Some star....

As Stella approached the corner to make her entrance, she cocked her glossy head at an angle so that her long yellow hair rippled flirtily down her slim, bare back. At thirty-two, she was still beautiful, and she knew it. Just as she knew how to use it.

"Fake it till you make it, baby," Johnny, her ex-manager, always said.

Fake it? For how much longer? In this business and this city, beauty was everything, at least for a woman.

Every day younger, fresher girls poured into Vegas, girls with big dreams just like hers. Johnny signed them all on, too.

Hips swaying, Stella moved like a feral cat, her lush, curvy, petite body inviting men to watch, not that there were many to do so tonight. There was a broad-shouldered hunk at the bar. He gave her the once-over. Her slanting, thickly-lashed, blue eyes said, "You can look, but keep your distance, big boy—this is my territory."

Johnny Silvers, her no-good ex-manager, who liked fast cars and faster women, had taught Stella how to move, how to walk, how to hold her head, how to look like a star—how to fake it.

Some star. The closest she'd come was to warm the crowd up before the real star came on stage.

Now she'd sunk to Harry's.

Harry's was a dead-end bar in downtown Vegas, a hangout for middle-aged retreads, divorcées, widowers, alcoholics, burned-out gamblers—a dimly lit refuge for the flotsam and jetsam who couldn't quite cut it in real life and were too broke to make their play in the hectic, brightly lit casinos on the strip. They were searching for new lives and new loves. Not that they could do more in Harry's than drown their sorrows and take a brief time-out before they resumed their panicky quests.

In a few more years, I'll be one of them, Stella thought as she grimly shoved a chair aside on her way to the bar.

Her slinky black dress was so tight across the hips, she had to stand at her end of the bar when she finally reached it. She'd put on a pound, maybe two. Not good, not when the new girls kept getting younger and slimmer.

Mo, the bartender, nodded hello and handed her her Saturday night special—water with a juicy lime hanging on the edge of her glass. She squeezed the lime, swirled the water in the glass. Wetting her lips first, she took a long, cool sip.

Aside from Mo and a single, shadowy male figure at the other end of the bar, Harry's was empty tonight. There wasn't a single retread. So, the only paying customer was the wide-shouldered hunk she'd seen come in earlier. She knew men. He was no retread.

There was a big arms-dealer conference in Vegas. For some reason, she imagined he might be connected to the conference. He was hard-edged. Lean and tall and trim. He had thick brown hair. She judged he was around thirty. Something about him made her think of the way Phillip looked in his uniform. Maybe it was the man's air of authority.

Just thinking about Phillip made her remember another bar seven years ago when she'd been a raw kid, singing her heart out, not really caring where she was as long as she could sing. She'd gotten herself in a real jam that night. Lucky for her, or maybe not so lucky as it turned out, Phillip Westin had walked in.

Just the memory of Phillip in that brawl—he'd been wonderful—made her pulse quicken again. It had been four drunks against one Marine, but a Marine whose hands were certified weapons. In the end Phillip had carried her out to his motorcycle, and they'd roared off in the dark. He'd been so tender and understanding that first night, so concerned about her. What had impressed her the most about him was that he hadn't tried to seduce her. They'd talked all night in a motel and had only ended up in bed a couple of days later.

The sex had been so hot, they'd stayed in that motel

bed for a week, making wild, passionate love every day and every night, even eating meals in bed, until finally they were so exhausted, they could only lie side by side laughing because they felt like a pair of limp noodles. When they'd come up for air, she'd said she'd never be able to walk again. And he'd said he'd never get it up again. She'd taken that as a challenge and proved him wrong. Oh, so deliciously wrong. Afterward, he'd asked her to marry him.

She'd said, "I don't even know you."

And he said, "Just say maybe."

"Maybe," she'd purred.

Maybe had been good enough for Phillip, at least for a while. He'd been living on his elderly uncle's ranch alone and supervising the cattle operation because his uncle, who had been ill, was in a nursing home. Everything had been wonderful between Celeste and Phillip until suddenly Phillip had received a call and had gone off on a mission. Alone on the ranch, she'd gotten scared and had felt abandoned and rejected just as she had when her parents had died.

If the days had been long without Phillip, the sleepless nights had seemed even longer. She hadn't known what to do with herself. She wasn't good at waiting or at being alone.

Then a pair of grim-faced Marines had turned up at the door and said Phillip was missing in action. She'd been terrified he was dead—just like her parents. A few weeks later Johnny had driven into town, promising he'd make her a star, saying Larry Martin, *the* Larry Martin wanted to produce her. He'd convinced her to go with him to Vegas. The rest was history.

All of a sudden her throat got scratchier. She knew

better than to think about the past. She swallowed, but the dry lump in her throat wouldn't go down.

How could she sing...tonight? To a man who reminded her of Phillip.

She asked Mo for another glass of water, but the icy drink only made her throat worse.

Did it matter any more how well she sang? This was Harry's. There was only one customer. She picked up her guitar and headed for the stage.

Just when she'd thought she couldn't sink any lower, she'd lost her job two weeks ago and the only guy Johnny could convince to hire her was Harry, a loser buddy of his.

"I can't work at a lowlife place like this," she'd cried when Johnny had brought her here and a cockroach had skittered across her toe.

"You gotta take what you can get, baby. That's life."

"I'm Stella Lamour. I've done TV. You promised I'd be a star."

"You've got to deliver. You're just a one-hit wonder. Wake up and smell the roses, baby."

She'd kicked the roach aside. "All I smell is stale beer."

"My point exactly, baby. You gotta fake it till you make it."

"I'm tired of faking it and not making it. You're fired, Johnny."

"Baby— Stella Lamour, the one-hit wonder." He'd laughed at her. "All right. Fire me. But take the job, baby—if you wanna eat."

She'd taken the job, but every night it was harder to pretend she would ever make it as a singer.

Now, Stella turned on the mike and got a lot of back

feed. When she adjusted it, and it squealed again, the broad-shouldered man at the bar jammed his big hands over his ears but edged closer. Again, the way he moved, reminded her so much of Phillip, her knees went a little weak and her pulse knocked against her rib age. Oh, Phillip....

Don't think about the past or Phillip. Just sing.

Why bother? Nobody's listening.

"I'll start off with a little number I wrote," she purred to Mo and the man. "Back in Texas."

The customer stared at her intently as if he liked what he saw.

"I wrote this seven years ago before I came to Vegas." She fiddled with the mike some more, and then she began to sing, "Nobody but you/Only you/And yet I had to say goodbye…"

She forgot she was in Harry's. She was back on the ranch on Phillip's front porch where the air was hot and dusty, where the long summer nights smelled of warm grass and mesquite, and the nights buzzed with the music of cicadas.

"I thought love cost too much," she purred in the smoky voice she'd counted on to make her famous, to make her somebody like her mother had promised. "But I didn't know."

Then she realized she was in Harry's, and her failures made her voice quiver with regret. "Everywhere I go/There's nobody but you in my heart/Only you."

Somehow she felt so weak all she could do was whisper the last refrain. "And yet I had to say goodbye."

Phillip was the only good man, the only really good thing that had ever happened to her. And she'd walked out on him. Big mistake. Huge.

She'd wanted to make it big to prove to Phillip she

was as good as he was…that she wasn't just some cheap
tart he'd picked up in a bar and brought home and bed-
ded…that she was somebody…a real somebody he
could be proud of.

She frowned when she heard a car zoom up the back
alley. Oh, dear. That sounded like Johnny's Corvette
sportscar. The last thing she needed was Johnny on her
case. Sure enough, within seconds, the front door banged
open and Johnny raced through it on his short legs. His
thick, barrel chest was heaving. His eyes bulged out of
their deep, pouchy sockets. The poor, little dear looked
like a fat, out-of-shape rabbit the hounds were chasing,
but his florid face lit up when he saw her.

"Baby!"

Oh, no. He definitely wanted something!

"You and I are through," she mouthed.

Johnny lit a cigarette. Then his short, fat legs went
into motion again and carried him across the bar toward
her.

He was a heavy smoker, so running wasn't easy.
When he reached the stage, he gasped in fits and starts,
which made his voice even more hoarse and raspy than
usual.

"Take a break, baby…" Pant. Wheeze. "I've got to
talk to you." Puff. Puff.

Fanning his smoke out of her face, she turned off the
mike and followed him to her end of the bar.

Johnny ordered a drink and belted it down. He ordered
a second one and said, "Put some booze in this one, you
cheap son of a—"

"Johnny, you can't talk to Mo like—"

Mo slammed the second drink down so hard it sloshed
all over Johnny's cigarette. Mo was big. A lot bigger
than Johnny. He had a bad temper, too. His face had

darkened the way it did when he had an impossible customer and had to play bouncer. Stella was afraid he'd pound Johnny.

"Easy, Mo," she whispered, wondering why she was bothering to defend Johnny, who'd brought her so much bad luck.

Mo whirled and went to tend to his other customer.

Johnny lit another cigarette. "Thanks, babe." Wheeze. Gulp. "I need money fast."

"I don't get paid till Monday." She clamped a hand over her mouth. "It's none of your business when I get paid."

"I got you this great new gig. Your ship's about to come in. You gotta help me, baby."

"That's what you said when you stole my royalties to buy those stolen tires and to pay your—"

"How was I— No-o-o. Baby!" Puff. Wheeze. "I borrowed a little cash to pay a few gambling debts. That's all! Honest! Now a couple of unreasonable guys are making insane demands on a poor guy trying to make his top girl a star—"

"I'm not your girl anymore!"

"Are you going to help me or not?" He was so charged with fear, his eyes stuck out on stems.

When would she ever learn? She hated herself for being such a softie.

"How much?"

"You've gotta big heart. You can't say that about many girls in Vegas."

Just as she slid her fingers into her bra and pulled out what little money she had, the front door banged open and two men in black, who instantly made her think of snakes—and she hated snakes—oozed inside.

"You'd better pay me back this time," she said.

"Sure, baby."

When the snakes yelled Johnny's name, he grabbed the money and ran out the back way, screaming, "She has it."

The two men raced past her after him. There was some sort of scuffle. Bodies thudded against a wall. The men shouted. Johnny squealed in pain. Then his super-charged, fancy black Corvette drove away fast, tires spinning gravel.

She was asking Mo for more water when the two snakes slithered quietly up behind her, grabbed her arms and shoved her against the bar.

"Hey, take your hands off me!"

Both of them had black, beady eyes. When their gazes drifted up and down her body, her heart raced.

"Johnny says you and he…. He says you've got our money." The man who held her had olive skin, a big nose and lots of pimples.

"I don't know what you're talking about." She began to shake. Everybody in Vegas knew guys like this didn't play around.

"Nero has methods to freshen a girl's memory," the taller snake said. "We're in the collection business. We specialize in gambling debts. Our customers lose. They borrow. If they don't want to pay, we motivate them. End of story."

The taller man was potato-pale. Gold-rimmed glasses pinched his nose as he stared at her breasts. "Name's The Pope. You're cute. You could work some of Johnny's debt off…if you get my drift."

"How much money does he owe you?" she whispered. Her heart was really knocking now.

The Pope named a preposterous sum that made her gasp.

"Johnny says you rolled the dice for him," The Pope said. "He says he gave you our money. Pay us, and we're out of here."

"I don't have it."

"Then get it. If you don't, we hurt you. Understand, sexy girl?" Nero said, pinching her arms.

She shivered. Oh, dear. They weren't kidding. Her eyes flew to the front door and to the back. She had to run. But before she took even one step, they read her mind.

"Oh, no you don't—" Nero grabbed her by the hair, intending to haul her out the door with him, when she bit his hand and then screamed for help.

On a howl of pain, he let her go. Since The Pope was blocking the exit, she ran toward the ladies' room. Nero would have chased her, but the wide-shouldered customer who reminded her of Phillip had sprung from the bar, stuck out a booted foot and tripped him.

"The lady said to let her go," said a hard voice as the short, dark thug went sprawling into chairs and tables that toppled on top of him.

"Stay out of this. The witch owes us money."

It was an exciting conversation. She would have loved to have stayed and listened, but it didn't seem smart to stick around. There was a window in the ladies' room just big enough for her to squeeze out of.

Once she made it to the ladies' room, the shouts from the bar got louder. Mo must have tackled the other guy.

"You a cop?" The Pope yelled.

"He's got cops' eyes. He moves like a cop, too—"

"We gotta blow this joint."

"What about her?"

"Later—"

As Stella stood on the toilet and opened the window,

she heard gunshots pop in the bar. In a panic, she shoved her guitar through the window. Then she scrambled out of it herself, only to lose her hold on the window frame and fall so hard, she nearly broke her ankle.

She got to her feet, straightened her ripped gown and then fluffed her hair. When she reached down to get her guitar, it wasn't there.

A large hand curved out of the darkness, and she jumped about a mile and then moaned in pain because she'd landed with all her weight on her bad ankle.

"Easy. I won't hurt you."

The big, handsome guy from the other end of the bar, the one who'd tripped Nero, held out her guitar.

She grabbed it and hugged it to her chest.

"Need a ride?" he asked in a hard, precise voice.

"As a matter of fact—" She blurted out her address.

"You can't go home. Can't stay in Vegas, either. Not with those guys after you. They'll kill you…or worse."

She gulped in a breath and then followed him to a sedan that was parked in the shadows. "But—"

"Do you think those guys are going to quit if you can't give them what they want?"

She swallowed.

"Honey, they know where you live."

"You're scaring me."

After he helped her into the front seat of the vehicle, he said, "Didn't your mama ever teach you never to ride with strangers?"

"I didn't have a mama."

He shut her door. "Everybody has a mama."

When he slid behind the wheel, she said, "I was five when she died."

"Too bad." He started the engine and revved it.

"You don't know the half of it. Foster homes. Cinderella. The whole bit. Only without the prince. But when I was little, I used to sing with my mama on stage. She told me I was going to be a star. And…and I believed her. But she died….'' Her voice shook. ''On a cheerier note, if you're a bad stranger, I can always beat you up with my guitar.''

He didn't laugh as they sped away. ''That'd be a waste of a good guitar.''

''Thanks for saving me.''

''So, where to?''

''The bus station.''

''And then?'' he persisted.

''Texas.'' She was surprised by her answer. *Texas?*

''Is that home?''

''Not exactly. But I have an old boyfriend with a hero complex.'' Phillip—he was the only man she knew tough enough to save her if those guys ever caught up with her. Oh, dear. Phillip—

''The poor sucker your song's about. You left him, didn't you?''

''He'll still help me.'' He would. She knew he would.

''What if he's married?''

''He's not.''

''And you know this how?''

She stared out her window at the bright glitter of Vegas. She wasn't about to admit she'd kept tabs by reading the Mission Creek newspaper online, so she bit her lip and said nothing.

When they got to the bus station, he got out with her and carried her guitar to the ticket window for her. Pulling out his wallet, he said, ''You gave your sleazy manager all your money, didn't you—''

''No, but I left my purse in my, er, dressing room.''

He counted out five one-hundred-dollar bills.

"I don't need nearly that much."

"It's a loan." He handed her his card.

"I'll pay it back. All of it. I really will...."

His face was grim as she read his card. "A.T.F. You're A.T.F." Her voice softened when she read his name. "Cole Yardley."

"Good luck," was all he said before he strode away.

"Thank you, Mr. Yardley," she whispered after him. "Thank you." Although he'd refused to open up, something about him made her long for Phillip.

She broke the first hundred and bought a one-way ticket to Mission Creek, Texas, where Phillip now lived. Phillip's uncle had died, and he'd inherited the ranch and made it his home.

Oh, Phillip—

Two

Mission Creek, Texas

It was 10:00 a.m. when the bus driver roared to a stop in front of the café in a swirl of dust under wide, hot, Texas skies. Not that the slim little girl behind him in what looked to be her mama's sophisticated black evening dress noticed. She was curled into a tight ball, her pretty face squashed against the back of her seat cushion.

Stella jumped when the driver shook her gently and said, "Mission Creek."

Not Stella anymore, she reminded herself drowsily. Not in Mission Creek. Here, she was Celeste Cavanaugh, a nobody.

"Didn't mean to scare you," the driver said as she rubbed her eyes and blinked into the white glare.

"Thanks. Give me a minute, okay?"

"Take your time. It's hot out there," he warned.

July. In Texas. Of course it was hot.

"No hotter than Vegas," she replied.

From the frying pan into the fire, she thought as she got up, gathered her guitar and stumbled out of the bus in her low-cut black dress and strappy high heels. For a long moment she just stood there in the dust and the baking heat. Then lifting her torn skirt up so it wouldn't drag in the dirt, she slung her guitar over her bare shoulder. Cocking her head at a saucy angle, she fought to pretend she was a star even though all she was doing was limping across an empty parking lot toward the café that was Mission Creek's answer for a bus station.

The historic square with its southwestern flair hadn't changed much. With a single glance she saw the quaint courthouse, the bank, the post office and the library. She was back in Mission Creek, the town she'd almost chosen to be her home. She was back—not that anybody knew or cared.

Inside the café, she hobbled to the ladies' room before she selected a table. It was a bad feeling to look in the mirror and hate the person she saw. The harsh fluorescent lighting combined with the white glare from the bathroom window revealed the thirty-hour bus ride's damage and way more reality than Celeste could face this early. Shutting her eyes, she splashed cold water on her cheeks and throat.

What would Phillip think when he saw her? Her eyeliner was smudged. What was left of her glossy red lipstick had caked and dried in the middle of her bottom lip. Her long yellow hair was greasy and stringy. She didn't have a comb, but she licked off her lipstick.

When she was done, she had a bad taste in her mouth, so she gargled and rinsed with lukewarm tap water. Oh, how she longed for a shower and a change of underwear and clothes.

Just when she'd thought she couldn't sink lower than Harry's, here she was at the Mission Creek Café in a ripped evening gown with a sprained ankle. Mission Creek Café. Phillip had brought her to lunch here once. The café was noted for its down-home country cooking. Oh, how Phillip had adored the biscuits.

Carbs. Celeste hadn't approved of him eating so many carbs.

She glanced at her reflection again. She was thirty-two. There were faint lines beneath her eyes. Faint.

Seven years later, and she was right back where she started. Still... Someday...

"I'm going to be big! A star! I am!"

A girl could dream, couldn't she?

The smell of biscuits wafted in the air.

Biscuits! In between dreaming, a girl had to eat. She was starving suddenly, and she had nearly four hundred dollars tucked snugly against her heart—more than enough for breakfast. After all, this wasn't the Ritz in Paris. This was Texas where carbs, and lots of them, the greasier the better, came cheap.

Celeste found a table in the back and ordered. When her plump waitress with the mop of curly brown hair returned with platters of eggs and mountains of hash browns and biscuits slathered in butter, Celeste decided to work up her nerve to ask about Phillip.

"More coffee, please," Celeste began.

"Sure, honey."

As the waitress poured, Celeste bit her lip and stared out the window. Not that there was much of a view other than the highway and a mesquite bush and a prickly pear or two.

Celeste could feel the woman's eyes on her. Still, she managed to get out her question in a small, shy voice.

"Does Phillip Westin still hang out at the Lazy W?"

The coffee pouring stopped instantly. "Who's asking?" The friendly, motherly voice had sharpened. The woman's black eyes seared her like lasers.

Celeste cringed a little deeper into her booth. "Can't a girl ask a simple question?"

"Not in this town, honey. Everybody's business is everybody's business."

"And I had such high hopes the town would mature."

"So—who's asking about Phillip?"

"Just an old friend."

"Westin has lots of lady friends."

"He does?" Celeste squeaked, and then covered her mouth.

"He meets them out at those fancy dances at the club."

"The Lone Star Country Club?"

"You been there?"

"A time or two."

"What's your name, honey?"

"Forget it."

"You're mighty secretive all of a sudden."

"Last I heard that wasn't a crime," Celeste said.

The waitress's smile died and she scurried off to the kitchen in a huff. Watching the doors slam, Celeste felt morose with guilt. She was running from killers, deliberately putting Phillip in danger. He'd moved on, made friends with real ladies at that fancy club he'd joined as soon as he'd moved here permanently.

He was wealthy. She was the last thing from a lady, the last thing he needed in his orderly life.

Her appetite gone, she set her fork down with a clatter.

What was the matter with her? Why had she argued with the waitress like that? It was just that she felt so lonely and scared and desperate, and so self-conscious about how cheap she looked. And then the woman had told her Phillip had lots of classy girlfriends.

Oh, why had she come here? Why had she ever thought— If she was smart, she'd catch the next bus to San Antonio. Then she'd lose herself in the big city.

Celeste should have known that wouldn't be the end of her exchange with the waitress. Not in a nosy little town like Mission Creek. Before her eggs had time to congeal, the plump woman was back with a cordless telephone and a great big gottcha smile.

"He's home," the waitress said.

"You didn't call him—"

The waitress winked at her and grinned slyly as she listened to Phillip.

"Oh, no.... You didn't. Hang up."

"She's got long yellow hair. It's sort of dirty. And a low-cut black dress with a rip up the left thigh. Nice legs, though. Sensational figure. And a great big shiny guitar that has a booth seat all to itself." She hesitated. "Yes, a guitar! And...and she's hurt... Her ankle...." Another pause. "What?" Again there was a long silence.

Celeste stared out at the prickly pear and chewed her quivering bottom lip. Then she buried her face in her hands.

"He wants to talk to you."

With a shaky hand, Celeste lifted the phone to her ear. "H-hello...?"

"Celeste?" Phillip's deep Marine Corps-issue voice sliced out her name with a vengeance.

"Phillip?"

"Mabel said you're limping."

"I'm fine. Never better."

"You're in some kind of trouble—"

She bit her lip and coiled a greasy strand of gold around a fingertip with chipped pearly nail polish. What was the use of lying to him? "I—I wish I could deny it."

"And you want me to rescue you...."

She swallowed as she thought of The Pope and Nero. If they followed her and killed Phillip, it would be all her fault.

Her throat burned and her eyes got hot. She squeezed them shut because the waitress was watching.

"How do you intend to play this? Sexy? Repentant? Do you see me riding into town on a white horse and carrying you out of the café in my arms?"

"Don't make this harder."

"What do you want from me then?"

Not to end up in some back alley with my skirt tossed over my head, my panties shredded and my throat slit.

"Just to see you," she said softly.

He laughed, but the brittle sound wasn't that deep chuckle she'd once loved. "You want way more than that and we both know it."

He knew how she hated that military, big man, know-it-all tone. She couldn't bear it any more than she could bear to answer him when he was feeling all self-righteous and judgmental.

"I wasn't born rich...like you.... Maybe if you'd gone through even half of what..." She stopped. That was a low blow. "I—I'm sorry."

For an instant—just for an instant—she saw her mother's white, lifeless face in her coffin and remembered how little and helpless she'd felt.

"Stay at the café. I'll send Juan to get you as soon as he gets back with the truck."

"Juan? I'd… I'd rather you came…."

But he didn't hear her heartfelt plea. He'd already hung up.

Thirty minutes later Phillip's ranch hand arrived in a whirl of dust. When Celeste saw him, she grabbed her guitar.

The waitress stared at the blowing dust and said to no one in particular, "It's awful dry out there. We could do with some rain."

Juan was short and dark, and dressed in a red shirt and baggy jeans coated with a week's supply of dirt. He didn't speak much English, and she didn't speak any Spanish. So she spent the ten-minute drive singing to the radio and watching the scenery go by. If you could call it scenery.

Unlike Vegas, south Texas was flat and covered with thorny brush. When they flew through the gate, Juan braked in front of a tall white house with a wraparound porch. Dust swirled around the truck and the wide front porch as he lit a cigarette.

She coughed. "Where's Mr. Westin?"

"Señor Westin?" Juan clomped up the stairs and pointed inside the house. Then he opened the screen door like a gentleman and beckoned for her to go inside. She nodded. Picking up her long skirt, she hesitantly stepped across the threshold into the living room.

The second she saw the burgundy couch she'd picked out at Sears, her heart began to beat too fast. Nothing much had changed. The same easy chair she'd bought for Phillip still squatted in front of the television set. Maybe the set was a little larger. She wasn't sure.

She knew her way around the house, not that she intended to explore the rooms in the house she'd once called home.

The Lazy W had been a rundown ranch Phillip had visited most summers as a kid. He'd grown up loving it. As an adult, he'd helped his uncle out when he'd been unable to do the work himself. Then a few years back, his elderly uncle had died and left him everything including the ranch.

Phillip had told her several of his friends who'd served under his command in the 14th Unit of the U.S. Marine Corps lived nearby, too. The guys had all belonged to the Lone Star Country Club, so Phillip had joined because they'd told him that's where the prettiest girls in town were. Apparently when the 14th unit was off duty, their favorite sport was chasing women.

Once a Marine, always a Marine, she thought grimly as she set her guitar down by the front door. Oh, dear, now that she was inside, it was all coming back to her. She'd been so crazily in love with Phillip, but at the same time, she'd wanted to be a star for as long as she could remember. Loving Phillip had only made her want it more. She'd wanted to be somebody…somebody special enough for Phillip to love on an equal footing, a somebody like her beautiful mother.

The two obsessions had fought within her. She'd felt deliriously happy when she was in Phillip's arms, and then the minute he'd gone off to war she'd felt scared and trapped. Then he'd gone missing.

How long did a woman wait for a man missing behind enemy lines? Her fear that he'd been dead, like her parents, had driven her mad. She'd felt as if she'd be a nothing forever if she didn't do something besides wait at the ranch. These very walls had seemed to close in on her like a prison. She'd had to run. She'd had to, but Phillip hadn't seen it that way.

When he'd turned up alive and called her, she'd been overjoyed. She'd wanted to see him so badly, to tell him about recording her first song, the song he'd inspired.

Oh, why hadn't he listened? Why hadn't he been able to understand? All he'd understood was that she'd left him.

"But I didn't know you were coming back! I thought you were dead!" she'd cried over and over again.

He hadn't listened. He'd believed the worst of her.

Now she was back in Phillip's living room. How would he treat her? Was he in love with someone else?

"Phillip," she cried, suddenly wanting to stop the bittersweet memories as well as her doubts about the wisdom of coming here.

"Phillip?"

He didn't answer.

Was she really so washed up she no longer had a chance to make it as a country-western star? Should she just give up and settle for some ordinary life filled with babies and chores with some ordinary man? Not that she'd ever thought of Phillip as ordinary.

She wandered into his kitchen. Dishes were piled high in the sink. She didn't have to answer all life's questions today. All she had to do was to convince Phillip to help her until she could find a job and could get back on her feet. He knew people. Maybe he could even get her a job if he wanted to. The Phillip she remembered liked to help people. Surely he'd help her. Even her. Surely—

"Phillip?"

Again, he didn't answer, but when she stepped into the hall, she heard his shower running. At the sound, she almost stopped breathing. Paralyzed, she stood outside his bedroom door until the water was turned off, and she heard the same old pipe that had always moaned groan and rumble. The shuddering sound broke the tension and she laughed.

They'd made love in that shower more times than she could count. She leaned against the wooden wall behind her and fought against the memories.

"Phillip?" she called again just so he wouldn't stomp out into the hall naked.

"Just a minute."

His deep, sexy baritone sent a shiver down her back, and that was before he stepped out of his bedroom into the hall in skintight, faded jeans that weren't zipped all the way up, rubbing his thick, dark hair with a white towel.

Oh, dear, he looked so good, and she was so grimy. She wished her mouth didn't taste so stale.

He tossed the towel back into his bedroom. She'd forgotten that when his dark hair was wet, it had a tendency to curl.

Her eyes fastened on his brown, muscular chest and flat belly, on the whorls of black hair running up and down his lean frame, before roving hungrily back to his rugged face.

Oh, dear. He'd stayed in shape. But, of course, he would. Phillip had the Marine Corps can-do, will-do, damn-it-to-hell-and-back attitude. He was disciplined, focused. He could make a plan and stick to it.

Not like her, who dreamed and wanted and then sometimes got lost in the day-to-day problems that came with living. Things that needed doing didn't always get done, and things she enjoyed doing were savored instead. She tended to drift and get nowhere or go hysterical and do nothing to solve her problem. She could waste days paralyzed by a mood. Which was why she'd landed on his doorstep without a dime of her own and looking even cheaper than the first night they'd met.

Some homecoming.

And Phillip? He was as handsome as ever, dangerously so. His mouth was wide and hard, his lower lip as sensuously kissable as ever. Oh, dear, she felt the old familiar ache to press her lips to his. He'd been so good at kissing, too. Too good.

Seven years on the ranch working outside had hardened his face and etched lines beneath his eyes and around his shapely mouth. He looked older, harsher, and yet...and yet he was still her Phillip.

Her Phillip? Don't be ridiculous!

He hadn't shaved yet, so his square jaw was covered with black bristles that made him look tough and virile and good enough to eat. Used to, he'd let her shave him in the shower before they'd made love.

Quit thinking about "used to."

When her eyes rose to his, he flushed. She felt her own skin heat when she realized he was staring at her breasts.

"I—I didn't have time to buy new clothes."

"How come you left Vegas in such a hurry?"

Her eyes widened in blank shock. The last thing she could tell him was the truth. He'd really despise her. Oh, why hadn't she checked into a motel and freshened up? Why hadn't she given herself a day to get her story together, a day to buy clothes and makeup?

Because unlike him, she wasn't a planner. Besides, she'd been too hysterical.

Instantly his silver eyes went opaque, and he met hers unsmilingly as he waited for her answer that didn't come. Suspicious, his carved face was a mask of military, tough-guy expressionlessness. Not by so much as a flicker of a black eyelash did he reveal that the sight of her in his hall looking weak and helpless and yet sexy and wild in a slinky black gown ripped to the thigh might disturb him.

His hard gaze returned to her breasts. The fact that he couldn't take his eyes off her body made her feel a little better. Even though she felt shyly nervous that he still found her desirable—she still felt better. Which was ridiculous. She wasn't here for sex or love or anything like that. She didn't want him wanting her. She didn't!

Liar.

"I must look a terrible mess," she said with an air of innocence that was completely false. Idly she fluffed her hair.

"You look good," was all he said. But his voice was bitter.

He stepped into the light and she saw the deep cut on his cheek.

"You're hurt." She slid across the hall and raised her hand, intending to touch him.

"It's nothing," he snapped.

Still, she came closer. Before he could move, she had her hand on the hot, rough skin near the ugly wound, her fingers tracing its edges tenderly.

"Oh, Phillip...." There were tears in her voice. "What happened?"

"Don't!"

"Did you go off on some silly mission again?" she asked.

"As if you give a damn— I could've died for all you'd care."

She had cared, but better not to go there, she thought.

He grabbed her hand, intending to push her away, but

the minute he touched her, she went strangely breathless. So did he.

Their eyes met, locked. On a raw, tortured note he whispered her name and she whispered his back, her voice as tremulous and lost as his.

Then it was as if they were caught in a spell. Some power outside of them and yet a part of them took over. Before she could stop herself, or he could push her away, she flung herself toward his hard, powerful body. Then she was in his arms, hugging him, clinging with a strength she hadn't known she possessed.

She felt so safe in his arms, so safe and protected after being so afraid. She melted against him like a frightened kitten shaping itself into a warm lap.

His skin was hot, so hot, burning up, and he smelled deliciously of shampoo and soap and yet of real man, too. Again, she remembered those long-ago romps in the shower.

"Hold me," she whispered. "Just hold me. It's been way too long."

He hesitated. Then he groaned and his arms wrapped her in a fierce embrace.

"How did I ever leave you? How?" she whispered. "How? Oh, Phillip, I thought you were—"

"Don't!"

He stiffened. Beneath her ear, his heart slammed in hard, furious strokes. The violent thudding thrilled her. So he wasn't immune to her any more than she was immune to him. He wasn't.

Not that she cared. Not that she could let herself care. She wanted to be a star. Not some rancher's wife in this hellish desert where it almost never rained unless a hurricane roared across the Gulf. Not the wife of some ex-

Marine who might go away to fight and die. Yet she clung to him and kissed his throat.

The kiss proved to be too much for him. The minute her mouth touched his skin, he let out a savage rasp and pushed her away.

"Don't try that again," he said hoarsely in his cruelest Marine Corps voice. "Unless you intend to deliver the goods." His silver eyes stripped her.

"Oh…." She gasped.

He was breathing hard, too.

"Westin, you always wanted me as much as I wanted you, so why does that make me some cheap, sexy tart in your mind?"

"You know the rules. It's not like I made them up."

"What rules? Oh…." Her heart was pounding so fast she could barely breathe, and not from passion now.

"Men can screw around," he said. "Women can't."

"Oh…. I don't… That's a horrible thing to say…in general…and about me. I haven't…"

"You arrive at my doorstep half-naked…in a provocative gown somebody—let's cut the bull, a man probably—tried to tear off you in a bar."

"That's not what—"

"You throw yourself on me, using every cheap trick in the book, and you expect me to believe…"

"I tore my skirt on a window frame."

"Sneaking out of some man's bedroom?"

"Think that if you want to! You're as impossible as ever. As pigheaded…as…as… You don't listen. You think you know everything."

"I know you—Biblically." He laughed. "You're just the same, too."

If that remark made her even madder, his next comment was like a torch thrown onto a pool of gasoline.

"I picked you up in a barroom brawl. I should've known what you were like then. But you came on so soft and sweet and helpless, you fooled me."

"And because of that first night, you think you're better than I am. You always have, and you always will."

"What if I do?"

"I don't know why I came back here."

"Let me guess. You're in some kind of a jam. You probably need money."

"I need a decent job."

"Ha! Dressed like that?"

"Listen to me…please. Just listen."

"You thought I'd be easy pickin's, didn't you? Living out here? Alone? No woman? Well, you were right about one thing, honey. I still want you."

His voice was so hard and filled with hate, she gasped.

"Look at me," he said.

Unwillingly, she met his shrewd gaze and instantly felt stripped to the marrow. Oh, dear. She was afraid she was transparent as glass.

"You feel the same way. So, do you want to stand here and argue, or would you rather just cut this nonsense, and go to bed? But don't flatter yourself. This isn't about love. It's about sex. And money. I'll pay—" He flung her his sexiest, male grin.

Maybe he was a whole lot cuter, but in some ways he was as bad as Nero and The Pope!

But he was her last chance! She clenched her fists and bit her tongue until it bled. Killers, real killers, were after her. She had to focus on why she'd come to see this impossible man she'd once been so foolish to love. Her fury made it hard to remember that besides being an egotistical, macho, oversexed idiot, Westin had a good, dependable, fierce side, too.

Pursuing this particular battle to its conclusion wasn't smart. After all, she had a plan this time. Somehow she had to convince him to help her get a real job. For once, she had to be smart and stick to her plan.

He broke the silence by laughing at her again. "There's no reason to play hard to get, honey. The sooner you go to bed with me, the sooner you get what you really want."

She lifted her chin. His dark gaze made a connection that was way too powerful.

"So I amuse you?" she whispered. "The man I used to know helped people when they came to him in trouble. He didn't insult them and laugh at them and try to take advantage of them…sexually—"

"You conniving— Why are you really here? What do you really want?" he growled.

If only he'd stop looking at her like that. Her heart was still pounding. "Like I said, I need a decent job, a place to live," she persisted.

"Decent?" He wasn't touching her, but his eyes pulled her erotically.

"Is that so hard to believe?" she whispered.

"Simple ambitions for a woman like you. Used to, you wanted fame and fortune."

"Was that really so terrible, Phillip?"

"Do you still want to be a country-western star?"

She wasn't about to admit her dreams to him. In his awful mood, he'd just laugh at her again.

She notched her chin higher. "Would it make you happy to know I've had a few hard knocks and learned a few lessons?"

"Then? What do you want?"

In spite of herself, just being near him made her feel a deep aching need.

"You know people. Maybe you could get me on at the Lone Star Country Club. As a singer. Or even a hostess or a waitress. I need a job."

"You want a job? I'll give you a job."

"I won't go to bed with you for money! And that's final!" Her shaky voice probably gave her away. Was it just chemistry that pulled her to him?

"I need a housekeeper," he stated flatly.

"I don't believe that's what you really—"

"Hear me out. You played Cinderella in all those foster homes. You can live here and do the same for me."

"I don't think it's such a good idea—the two of us living here. Not when you just suggested we go to bed in such a sordid—"

"Don't act like you deserve better. Take it or leave it."

"You didn't used to be this hard," she said softly.

"Maybe I suffered a few hard knocks of my own. I nearly died in the Middle East."

"Oh, Phillip—" Her voice broke.

"Then I came home to marry the woman I loved. Only she'd run off with another man."

His gaze stayed on her face for a long, searching moment.

"I didn't run off with Johnny. It wasn't that way at all and you know it."

"No, I don't know it. How was it, then?"

"You wouldn't listen then."

"You were gone. That's all I know."

"Yes…." She cleared her throat. "And…and I'm sorry if I hurt you."

"You didn't— I don't give a damn about you anymore—understand."

He looked away and she suddenly realized how profoundly she'd hurt him.

"Oh, Phillip—"

He'd cared too much. That's why he hadn't come after her. She'd been so caught up in her own dreams and pain and self-doubt, so sure she'd had to prove herself to him, she hadn't really thought that someone as tough as he was might be as vulnerable and needy as she was. Well, it was too late now. He was hard and cold, and so set against her he was treating her as though she was some trashy stranger.

"What really happened to your face?" she whispered.

"I had an accident. I wasn't wearing a seat belt."

"You should be more careful."

"You gonna stay here and take care of me?"

"Not a good idea. I'm beginning to see we weren't really very good for each other."

"Yet you've come back?"

"Big mistake. I'll go. Forget I ever came…."

He didn't try to stop her when she turned to leave. At the door, she picked up her guitar, which felt as heavy as lead. As soon as she stepped off his front porch into the sun, she realized she was in the middle of nowhere. The sun was so hot, it felt about an inch off her bare shoulders. She felt weak and tired, so tired. So helpless and so hopeless.

With her turned ankle, she'd never be able to walk all the way back to town. Juan was nowhere in sight.

"How the hell do you think you'll get to town?"

She stiffened. No way was she going to beg. "I'll find Juan. He'll give me a ride back to town."

"He's out back."

When she headed out to the barn, she saw the buzzards, which meant there had to be a dead animal out in the pasture. Curious, she let herself through a gate to check on whatever was wrong.

The sun on her face and shoulders grew hotter by the minute, so hot she could almost feel her nose blistering. Holding up her hand to shield her face, she didn't have to walk far before she smelled the stench. Flies hovered above a cow that lay on it side, its belly bloated. Its legs stuck straight out. Black vultures whooshed excitedly around it when she walked up.

Oh, dear. The animal's eyes were gaping sockets. She was about to call for Phillip when a slip of fluttering white caught her attention. Somebody had nailed a note to the dead carcass.

Big block letters read, "You hurt my family, so now I will hurt yours."

She screamed. Then the thick smell of the barnyard and the stench of the dead cow combined with the heat and she felt nauseated. The world seemed to spin, and she grew so unsteady on her feet, she was afraid she'd fall.

Somewhere behind her a screen door slammed. Then The Pope and Nero were grabbing at her long hair.

"Phillip," she whispered groggily. "Save me! Don't let them—"

"Who, my darling— There's nobody here!"

"Thank goodness." Her eyelids felt incredibly heavy as she grabbed a fence railing. The sun burned her face and made her lips feel dry. The sky seemed to blacken. In a halting breath she whispered, "Phillip…."

"I'm here. Right here," he said huskily.

She shook her head back and forth. "Phillip— Phillip— No! Phillip doesn't want me."

Then she felt strong arms around her and her words

were muttered shudderingly against his thick, hard shoulder.

"Don't be too sure about that, honey," his gentle voice soothed.

She felt herself being lifted.

"Celeste...."

For a fleeting moment she realized she really was in Phillip's arms. Only the Phillip who held her now wasn't the harsh Phillip who despised her. No. This Phillip was the gentle, warrior giant she'd fallen in love with.

A weak smile formed at the edges of her lips as she whispered his name and begged him to save her. Then everything went black.

Three

───

When Celeste regained consciousness, she was in Phillip's bed and he was sitting beside her on the edge of the mattress.

"I'm sorry," he said.

"I'll stay," she whispered.

"Why?"

"Because I need a job. Any job. And I don't have anywhere else to go." Too proud to meet his eyes, she stared guiltily past his dark face until the bright window behind him began to swim. *Because I know you'll help me.*

"Don't cry," he murmured.

She brushed at her damp eyes. "Who's crying?"

He handed her his handkerchief.

She dabbed at her eyes. "I'm not crying!"

He laughed and touched her wet cheek with a blunt fingertip.

"I hate it when this happens." In spite of herself, she smiled at him.

"That's better," he whispered, his deep voice gentle. "For the record, I'm going to call the sheriff and get him to investigate the cow killing. I think I know who's behind this."

"Who—" She shivered guiltily at the thought of Nero or The Pope.

"This isn't about you," Phillip said. "It's about me and some unfinished business in Central America."

"Central America?"

"Never mind. Just be careful. Lock the doors when I'm gone and Juan's not around. I don't want anything to happen to you. I'd never forgive myself if my work endangered you."

"Your work?"

"Shh."

She gulped in a deep breath. He was so concerned for her, she felt ashamed she'd left Vegas with a pair of killers after her. Ashamed that all her dreams and hard work had left her worse off than before she'd started. She was touched that he was so selflessly eager to protect her. There was no way she could confess that she was probably endangering him.

"Thank you, Phillip. I won't stay long—I swear."

"Stay as long as you like," he said.

She yawned and closed her eyes. When she opened them again, he was gone. The shades were drawn and there was a box of clothes on the floor. He must have come in at some point when she'd been asleep. When she got up and knelt to open the box, all the clothes she hadn't taken with her seven years ago were inside.

He'd kept them…packed them away…all these years. Had he been waiting and hoping she'd come back?

"Oh, Phillip—"

Suddenly she almost hated herself. She was using him as a human shield. Maybe The Pope and Nero had followed her. Maybe they'd killed the cow.

Tell him. He deserves the truth. If you don't tell him— he'll be furious.

She pulled a thin white dress out of the box and held it against her body. Memories tugged at her.

They'd driven in to a posh shop in Corpus Christi one afternoon and he'd bought her several outfits shortly before he'd left for the Middle East. He'd liked this particular dress so much, she'd worn it out of the store with the tags still on it. He'd laughed and cut off the tags with his pocketknife. Then they'd driven out to Mustang Island and had gone for a walk on the beach. It had been early spring and the southeasterly breeze had been strong. She'd chased seagulls, her skirts swirling. He'd caught her, and they'd found a secluded spot behind the dunes and made love on their beach towels.

Fingering the tiny buttons, she began to shake as she remembered his fingers fumbling with each pearly stud as he'd undone them one by one. He'd been so clumsy, she'd had to help him.

"Oh, Phillip—" She buried her face in the soft white cloth, wishing it didn't remind her of how sweet life with Phillip had once been.

"I won't be staying long. I won't. I can't love him. I can't. I'll get myself back on track and he'll never have to know the whole truth. He doesn't still love me. I can't hurt him now."

She put Phillip out of her mind and took a long hot bath and washed her hair. After towel-drying her hair, she slipped into the white dress with the gleaming pearl buttons. It felt so good to be fresh and clean—to be home.

She turned in front of the mirror and the circular skirt floated around her legs. Then she stopped herself.

"This isn't home. I'm still going to be a star."

Was she really? Or had she just lived on dreams so long, she didn't know how to live any other way? Dreams kept her going. They made it possible for her to face the everyday pain and the hassles of life and find them bearable, made it possible for her to hold her head up even with killers tracking her.

She'd put Phillip in danger. Maybe she'd gotten his cow killed. Would she ever be worthy of a man like Phillip?

He thought he'd seen her at her lowest in the bar brawl. He didn't know. She hadn't told him near everything about what she'd endured in those foster homes. Never once had she told anybody how often she'd had to change homes because her new "father" had started looking at her wrong. And that had meant she'd had to change schools.

So often had she changed schools, she hadn't been able to make friends with the good kids, and, of course, she'd fallen behind in her schoolwork. Once she'd even flunked a grade, which had made the kids, at least the ones she'd admired, believe she was stupid.

The spring of her junior year in high school, she'd painted her lips with bright red lipstick and auditioned for the talent show. Only when she'd stood on that stage had the other kids begun to think she was special. When she'd sung for them, she'd felt reborn, as though she was a whole new person. If she hadn't had that special gift she'd inherited from her mother, she would have stopped believing in herself a long time ago. Every time she remembered standing on that stage behind her mother as a little kid, she knew she couldn't quit.

The days passed. Before she knew it a whole week had flown by. Not once had Phillip hit on her.

She relaxed a little and began to let herself notice him a little more. She tried hard not to smile at him when he said something. Some part of her wanted to get up first thing and make his coffee. But she didn't.

Life as his housekeeper soon became routine. The work itself might be the same everywhere, but Phillip's being around spiced up the most mundane activities. Not that he made any more overt moves.

Still, there were more than a few awkward moments, especially at first, such as when he'd asked her where she wanted to sleep, and she'd eyed his bedroom door, hesitating a second or two before choosing the last bedroom down the hall instead of his, the one they'd once shared.

All he'd said was, "Okay," but his eyes had grown dark and cold, and the military mask had fallen into place when she'd carried her box of clothes from his bedroom down the hall.

Being a Marine, he tried to run his home the way he might run a military base. Maybe that worked when she wasn't around, but she wasn't about to play the grunt to his Lt. Col. Westin. On the first morning after she'd bathed and slipped into her soft white dress, he'd caught her on the back porch when she was towel-drying her hair and had started off with a long list of orders.

"I want you up at 0600 sharp," he'd barked.

"This is a home not some Marine camp," she'd replied.

Laughing at his audacity, she'd saluted him with her

left hand. "I never did get those big old numbers—
0600? Translation, please!" She'd wadded his list of
chores and stuffed it down the scooped neckline of her
soft white dress and into her bra.

"Six a.m. Sharp."

"You can't be serious," she'd said, aware of his silver
eyes lingering on her hand between her breasts. "Only
lunatics or maniacal Marines get up at such an ungodly
hour."

"You didn't even read my list—"

"I know how to keep house! You don't have to tell
me what to do!"

"You could have at least read—"

"Didn't anybody in colonel school ever teach you to
delegate?"

"There's no such thing as colonel school."

"Maybe there should be."

She'd made a habit of sleeping through the alarm he
set for her every night just as she had made a habit of
ignoring the long lists of chores he left on the kitchen
table every morning. Instead, she did what she thought
needed doing, which was more than he ever saw. Nat-
urally, there were some resulting fireworks. He had
started in on her that first night.

No sooner had they sat down to supper than Phillip
had started shooting blunt questions at her, like, "Did
you do…?" Then he'd systematically gone down his
list, which he knew by heart and she hadn't bothered to
read, unerringly selecting the tasks she'd neglected to
do, such as keeping the doors locked all the time, instead
of the chores she'd done.

"Did you iron my shirts?"

"In this heat?"

"Why isn't my bed made?"

"It isn't? Why, I went in—"

She'd stopped. No way could she admit that when she'd lifted his pillow, she'd thought of him lying there and cupped it against her face to breathe in his tangy, male scent. Then the memories of them together in his bed had flooded her and she'd run.

Blushing, she'd toyed with a strand of her hair. Her tongue seemed to stick itself to the roof of her mouth.

He'd turned a little red, too. "Okay. Okay. Forget the bed."

"I can if you can." She'd hardly breathed.

"What about my clothes in the hamper?" he'd growled.

"The...hamper's in your bedroom, too," she'd whispered.

"Oh."

"I—I'll do them tomorrow...if you'll bring the hamper to the laundry room."

"Did you—"

"Phillip, did you memorize your old list—"

"I know what I wrote down—"

This was bad.

Cocking her head saucily, she'd shaken her yellow curls. To gain time she'd fluffed them around her shoulders. "Of course, I didn't do those silly things on your silly list. There were way too many. If you knew anything—you'd know no woman could have done all that in one day—"

"Of course you didn't? What kind of employee are you?"

"The same kind of boss you are. A good boss would praise me for making the kitchen look so wonderful. I rearranged—"

"You hid everything. I couldn't even find a spoon."

"It's called finding a place for things and putting them where they belong. I even dusted behind the canisters and…and I bleached the sink."

He'd glared at her.

"That wasn't on my list."

"The porcelain was all yellow and stained." She'd smiled.

"Don't forget this is my house. You work for me."

"I wouldn't have to if you'd help me get a real job."

He'd jabbed at his eggplant. Then he'd begun to eat in silence. When he helped himself to seconds, she'd beamed. "How's the eggplant Provençale by the way?"

"Eggplant? I don't eat eggplant!"

"Then why is yours all gone?"

He'd eyed his clean plate with amazement. "Because…because I was starving, that's why!"

"Because you liked it," she'd amended gently.

"I wrote steak at the top of my list."

"Have you been listening to me at all? I didn't read your stupid list. I don't do lists."

"I wanted steak."

"Hardening of the arteries," she'd murmured. "Ever hear of that?"

"What?"

"Men in this country eat way too much red meat. You probably eat too much steak. At your age—"

"You work for me."

"Aye. Aye." She'd saluted him with her left hand.

Before he thought, he'd almost saluted her. Then he'd clenched his fingers into a fist and slammed it on the table. "You haven't done one single thing I wrote down today."

"Because you're not a housekeeper or a cook. You

don't think about your health. In short, you don't think like a woman…''

''Thank God!''

''You don't have the least idea what to put on my list. You write down all these silly things that no woman in her right mind would ever do.''

''Don't be absurd. You work for me—a man, in case you haven't noticed.''

''Oh….'' She'd slanted her long-lashed eyes his way. Then she'd batted them and given him a seductive smile. ''Oh, I see. This isn't about your list. You're just sulking because I don't want to share your bedroom.''

''The hell I am.''

''Then fire me.''

''And you'd go?''

''All you have to do is get me a real job.'' She'd flashed him her most brilliant smile. ''But if you won't get me a real job, as a tiny concession…because you're so stubborn, we'll have steak tomorrow.''

''I'm stubborn?''

She'd giggled. ''But no more than five ounces of red meat.''

''You're impossible.'' But he'd grinned back at her.

''Look who's talking.''

''You'll really cook steak?''

Over dessert, which was strawberries and fat-free, sugar-free vanilla ice cream, she'd said, ''Since you're not going to fire me…''

''It doesn't take much for you to get cocky—''

''Which is a trait I share with you.''

She knew she shouldn't tease him. It made her remember how wonderful loving him had been. To break the spell, she'd sat up straighter and said, ''Phillip, I need money.''

"I knew it."

"Could I have an advance against my paycheck?"

"An advance? Already?"

"It's important…or I wouldn't ask."

"How much?"

She'd named the exact amount she needed to pay Cole Yardley.

Phillip had given her a sharp look, but he hadn't asked what the money was for.

"I owe somebody," she'd blurted, on the defensive because she could tell he was suspicious. "That's all."

"All right. We'll leave it at that."

The next morning, she'd gone to the bank and the post office and sent Mr. Yardley a five-hundred-dollar money order.

In a month, Phillip calmed down. He stopped writing lists. Maybe she'd worn him down. Or maybe he liked the way she did things more than he would admit. She wasn't sure. When there were no more dead cows, she quit worrying that The Pope and Nero had discovered her hiding place.

Growing up in so many homes, she'd learned there were lots of ways to run a household, and if she was going to be the woman of this house, especially when Phillip was a rancher and could pop in at any time, she had to do things her way. No woman in her right mind would let the man have the upper hand in such a situation.

Last night he'd almost said he preferred her menus to his—before he'd caught himself. She cooked lots of vegetables. If she'd left things to him, he would have eaten steak and potatoes every night.

Once things were easier between them, and she'd

taught him she wasn't some grunt he could boss around, new tensions, or maybe the same old tensions, began to build inside her. When they were in the same room, and he followed her with his eyes, she would feel the little hairs on the back of her neck stand up. She would blush and smile at him shyly, and he would look away too quickly.

To avoid such scenes, she kept away from him. When he watched television in the living room, she stayed in the kitchen and read by herself. Not that she could totally ignore him even there. He'd laugh and she'd look up from her woman's magazine and think about him in those ways she didn't want to think about him.

He was so big and broad-chested and tanned. And his mouth. Oh, dear. That warm, gorgeous, delicious-looking mouth of his. Just the thought of his mouth tickling her skin made her knot her hands in her lap and made her body get hot all over. Yes, even in the kitchen all by herself, knowing he was nearby made her edgy and restless and somehow unfulfilled. Before, he'd been affectionate all through the day. Seven years ago he used to come up behind her without warning and she'd feel his fingers at her nape and then his lips.

Now, nights when he didn't come home at his usual hour, she would run to the front door or watch the phone, waiting for it to ring. And all the time an ache in her stomach would worsen as she wondered where he was.

She'd worry herself into a headache. Maybe he'd had an accident and had forgotten to put on his seat belt again. Maybe he'd fallen off the tractor or been gored. Maybe whoever had killed that cow had attacked Phillip. Not that Phillip ever told her his plans. Not that his whereabouts were any of her business. After all, they weren't married. They weren't even lovers. All they were was boss and employee. And as the weeks passed, both were more determined than ever that the other understood that. It was as if they'd drawn lines in the sand and dared one another not to step across. But she worried about him. She couldn't stop herself. And she thought about him constantly. She even sang about him.

When her chores were done, and she had nothing to do, she would go to her bedroom or sit on the front porch with her guitar and write songs. The best ones were always about Phillip. How could that be when he was her boss?

What was she doing here? Was she crazy?

When Phillip was away, she taped the songs and mailed them with a letter to a hot new producer, Greg Furman, in Nashville. Not that Furman ever wrote her back. Even so, she always felt a little guilty, as though she was going behind Phillip's back, as though she should share everything in her heart and soul with him.

But her career was none of his business. What were they to each other, really? She was his maid and that was hardly the career she'd had in mind. Constantly, she had to work to remind herself that this wasn't her home, that Phillip wasn't her husband or even her lover, and that he never would be. But she thought about him when she was in bed, and she dreamed about him when she slept.

She would wake up and tell herself she owed him nothing. Nothing but her friendship! She would tell herself that the next night she would refuse to think about him or dream about him, that she was her own person, and as such, she had to get her career back on track—as soon as possible. And yet...

And yet the very next night, when she was alone in her narrow little bed again and he was such a short distance down the hall in his big double bed they'd shared and made passionate love in, staying in his house even for a few months would seem like a big mistake. A board would creak outside her room and she'd nearly jump out of her skin, thinking it might be Phillip at her door. Hoping it was, her heart would beat faster. She'd imagine his hand on her doorknob, and a bolt of heat would course through her. She'd sit up shivering expectantly. Then she'd realize he wasn't there. She'd wrap her arms around herself and remember how it used to be when they'd lain in bed in each other's arms.

Even when they hadn't been making love, they'd never kept to their own side of the bed. He'd held her close all night. Lying like that in his arms, she'd never felt so safe and so protected, at least, not since her mother had died and left her alone.

"Oh, Phillip, Phillip, you drive me so crazy! What is wrong with me?" The harder she fought not to care about him, the more involved she became.

One day when Celeste was out in the rocking chair, playing her guitar and singing on the porch, Phillip, who was supposed to be out in some far-flung pasture, stalked around the back of the house in a freshly starched white shirt and a pair of pressed jeans. He appeared so suddenly, he caught her singing about him.

"I didn't know I was on the road to nowhere when I left you..."

Rocks spun from under his big boots as he came to a standstill in the gravel beside the back porch. "Celeste..."

Instantly she stopped singing, the last word tumbling out of its phrase as if into a deep pool of clear green water. "You-u-u...."

"You singing about me, girl?"

For no reason at all, she couldn't let go of his silver gaze. She wasn't sure she'd ever noticed before that his pale gray irises were ringed with black.

"Go on," he whispered, looking up at her. "You're great."

She plucked a guitar string, nervous at the thought of him listening. For a tough guy, he sure had pretty eyes.

"Go on—please. You have a beautiful voice."

She leaned back in the rocker and resumed playing. "The lights ahead were so bright, they blinded me…"

He seemed to hold his breath as he looked up at her and listened without comment.

"I couldn't see that fame and fortune weren't enough/ that without you, I'm on the road to nowhere."

"Did you write that?" he whispered.

She nodded.

"You still want to be a star?"

"This star crashed and burned."

"What happened to you in Vegas?" He moved toward the porch.

"I don't want to go there. Please don't ask." Just the thought of Nero and The Pope still scared her to death.

She averted her eyes, so Phillip wouldn't see the guilt she felt for putting him in danger.

"You're a wonderful singer and a wonderful writer," he said softly, placing a booted foot on the first step.

"I was a one-song wonder, remember?" She bit her lip and shut her eyes.

"Celeste—don't be so hard on yourself."

"It's the truth."

"Maybe it doesn't have to be."

"What are you saying?" She couldn't believe he was encouraging her. "Dinner's ready," she said.

"I don't give a damn about dinner."

He sprang up the stairs to the porch two at a time and sank down on his knees beside her rocking chair. She began to shake a little. Did he have to come so close? Did he know what he did to her?

Her palms grew damp and she wiped them on her jeans, but there was no way she could calm the giddy wildness that made her heart flutter.

"If you've got talent the way you do, can you really get it out of your system?" he persisted gently. "Can a dream like that die?"

"I don't want to talk about…"

"What will happen to you if you let it die?"

"I can't believe you're…" She didn't trust herself to go on. His sensitive questions as well as his concern shook her more than anything he could have done or said. "Marines don't talk about dreams."

"Yeah. We're natural-born killing machines."

"Look. You were Alpha Force."

"I know what I was. I'm other things, too."

"I—I didn't mean…"

"Yeah, you did—"

"I'm thirty-two," she said.

"Dreams don't die because you get to a certain age. Thirty-two is young."

"People grow up," she whispered.

"Do they?"

"They're supposed to." Talking about her music made her uncomfortable. "Aren't you still the Marine who wants to serve his country, and you don't care who you have to kill or if you die doing it?"

"I retired. My Marine buddies say I've gone through my nine lives, that I'd better find the right woman, a churchgoing woman and settle down."

His teasing smile gave her a warm buzz. Before she thought, she grinned, too.

"Churchgoing, huh? That's not me, is it?" She blushed. "They're right, you know. You should."

"I don't go to church much—especially since you came home."

Home. This isn't home. Why was that so hard for her to remember?

"What are you saying?" she whispered.

"I'm wondering why you came back to me."

"Back to Texas," she corrected. "Not back to you."

"You knew I was here. Admit it."

Suddenly she started rubbing her arms as if there was a chill in the air.

"Let's quit fooling ourselves," he said, his eyes dark and hot.

"Phillip—"

She stood and set her guitar in the rocker before backing toward the kitchen door.

He crisscrossed his muscular forearms. "Damn it, I've tried not to look at you."

"Me, too," she whispered, her voice thready.

"And I've tried to avoid you."

"Me, too."

He scowled at her. "But you consume me."

"I—I don't want to talk about this, either." Jerkily she grabbed at the screen door.

"Good. I don't want to talk—period." His hand seized hers. "At night I lie awake," he began, his voice rough and strange.

So did she. Not that she could admit it.

"Don't," she whispered even though all her senses were clamoring for him to keep talking.

"I still want you," he rasped, sliding his work-roughened palms up her bare arms and making her gasp.

"Phillip, I..."

"Why the hell do you write songs about me, if it's really over for you?"

"I... That song wasn't really about you."

"Right." He laughed harshly. "You never were much of a liar. That's one of the things I liked about you. You used to tell me everything. About those homes you lived in. About feeling so loved on that stage with your mother. I wanted to make you feel that loved. I tried so damn hard."

"Oh, Phillip. I know you did, and I did feel loved."

He sighed.

She bit her lip. "Until you went away."

He'd made her feel so loved, so adored. Then he'd gotten that phone call in the middle of the night and he'd gone off to the Middle East and gotten himself captured. She stopped herself from reliving the past.

Oh, dear. It was all such a long time ago. Why were her feelings about him still so intense? Why?

Phillip seemed to sense her vulnerability and pressed closer. "Just one kiss," he whispered, clutching her hand again, pulling her into his body. "Is that so much to ask? One kiss? Just to see if you still taste the same. I've got to know."

"Maybe ignorance is bliss."

"Ah—bliss."

His eyes were on her lips, and she was staring at his mouth, too.

When he moved toward her with a predatory male gleam in his eyes, she didn't back away. He let her hand drop and began to stroke her hair and neck soothingly.

She was trembling from his touch, and he was on fire with need.

His skin was so hot, she caught fire, too. He lowered his lips to her temple and rained hot nibbles in her hair that sent little jolts of fire all through her. Without thinking she buried her face in the hollow of his warm throat and weakly kissed his mad pulse beat. He threw back his head, his gray eyes dark and wild with desire.

After a few moments, holding each other made them want more. So much more. Blindly his mouth sought hers.

Blindly, she opened her lips to his. Their mouths clung; their tongues mated. He groaned. His large hands pressed into the small of her back, shaping her against his muscular torso. He was thick and hard against her thigh.

She wanted to unfasten his belt buckle, to rip it out of the denim loops, to unzip him…to…to… And all the time as their lips devoured each other, their hunger grew until she could barely breathe.

There. This. She sighed heedlessly as the tumult from kissing him and holding him possessed her utterly. *This is what I want. What I've wanted every night when I've lain awake. This. You!*

"Oh, Phillip—"

"You're still a perfect fit," he muttered raggedly, his scorching mouth against her hot cheek now.

"So are you."

"Wrap your legs around me."

"Out here?" she murmured.

"Why the hell not? There's nobody to see us."

"Slow down. Maybe because I'm not done kissing you yet," she replied.

"So you want more kisses?"

"Maybe just a few more." She giggled primly, eyeing his lips.

Oh, that mouth of his. That beautiful, beautiful mouth!

His lips claimed hers greedily again, as if he, too, were starved for her loving and would never get his fill. Soon his kisses grew more urgent and she was gasping with such intense pleasure her feelings terrified her.

The dusty cactus and mesquite stretching toward the endless, flat horizon seemed to whirl around her. Soon she felt so dizzy and faint she could barely stand.

"No," she moaned, gripping him by the waist. "We…we can't do this."

"Wrap your legs around me the way you used to," he ordered.

Every sense in her female being went on red alert. But she said, "I'm just your housekeeper now."

"You're way overdue for a promotion. I have a job in mind you're way better qualified for."

"Oh, Phillip— We've got to stop! Really!"

"Really?" he murmured, pressing her closer. He stared at her, his gaze drifting from her lips to her breasts, to her belly and lower…

She had to stop him.

Her hands fell from his neck and pushed against his massive chest. For a minute or two, he resisted.

"If we let this get out of hand, we'd only end up hurting each other."

He didn't say anything, so it was up to her to do the smart thing.

"Find that nice, churchgoing girl," she whispered, lifting her gaze to his. "She's not me, and we both know it."

"Are you really so sure?" he muttered, wrapping an arm around her waist and tugging her toward the door.

She liked being in his arms. She liked it too much. "We tried before. I loved the sound of the guitar and the glitter of bright lights, and you loved the sound of bullets."

"Not anymore. I know what I want now, and it's not war or death. But what do you want, Celeste? You came home. To me. Why?"

"You keep saying that…like it means something. It doesn't."

"Maybe it does."

"This isn't home…. At least, it's not my home."

He let her go. "Maybe it could be. You could stay and keep writing your songs."

"Could I?" She stared at her guitar in the rocker and hugged herself. "Yes, I always write songs wherever I am. I can't seem to stop." She fought to calm herself. It was unbearably exciting to even think she might have him and her music, too. But how? How? He'd said dreams didn't die, and he was right. Hers hadn't. But wasn't that the problem for them?

Besides, because of her early losses and pain, she couldn't trust him or herself or their love. Some part of her thought it would all go away. Still, she couldn't stop her feelings for him any more than she could stop the music in her soul. It was as if he'd claimed a part of her, and she'd never be free again.

If she let this go any further, they'd fall in love all over again. Someday she would have to choose. If they stopped now, maybe they wouldn't have to hurt each other again.

She studied the hollows beneath his cheekbones. She caught the faint scent of laundry detergent from his freshly washed shirt. She wanted him so much, she ached. And she loved the wild loneliness of his ranch.

Maybe he really was tired of war. Well, she was definitely tired of lousy gigs and cheap apartments with rented furniture. It was so nice here with him where she felt safe, where he made her feel beautiful and special. But was he enough for a girl like her? Wouldn't her dream always be there between them? Would the bright lights beckon her again after a few more months?

Confused and lonely as she was, it would be too easy to lead him on, to live here under his protection until she felt safe and had enough money to pursue her real dream, which had always been singing. But she wanted him. Oh, how she wanted him.

She stared at his dark, tanned face, into his wild silver eyes that carved out her soul. In this moment she wanted him even more than she could ever imagine wanting to be a star. But when he leaned down and tried to kiss her again, she shook her head sadly and bit her lip.

Lifting her guitar from the rocker, she began to sing to him, "Without you, I'm on the road to nowhere..."

"So that's how it is!"

"That's how it has to be," she whispered.

"Maybe we're both on the road to nowhere." He lashed out, suddenly angry at her rejection. "When you came back—you put me in hell. Did you know that? You think I'm made of iron? That I'm some kind of cold-blooded killing machine?"

"I didn't mean for it to be like that."

"You're so damned beautiful. So damned sweet. You! It's always about you! Stay away from me—you hear!"

He stomped into the house and slammed the door so hard the whole house shook.

"I've been trying to!" she yelled.

Alone on the porch, she felt as if the big desolate

landscape had swallowed her alive. She sucked in a breath. Panic tore through her.

"I—I didn't want to hurt you. That's the last thing I wanted." She went to the door and then clenched her fingers and sank to the porch floor. "Why do we always end up hurting each other?"

She put down her guitar and fought her tears.

Four

Phillip turned the window unit in the kitchen up full-blast to drown out Celeste's plaintive voice. When he could still hear her singing, he splashed two shots of bourbon onto ice in a short glass and quickly gulped it down, coughing when the stuff burned like acid. Not that he felt it as he began to pace.

A message light blinked on his answering machine. Welcoming any distraction, he strode over to the phone and punched the play button. Justin Wainwright's deep voice came on instantly. Justin was the local sheriff, and with Phillip's help, he was investigating the cow killing that had terrified Celeste.

"Thanks for all your input, Westin. Afraid I still can't pin that dead cow to the Gonzalez character you mentioned even though the FBI is taking your concerns very seriously. The feds are sending an agent to check out our theory about Gonzalez smuggling guns out of Mission Creek—''

Phillip deleted the message, turned the machine off and moved toward the air conditioner so he could watch Celeste through the window. Her golden head was lowered over her guitar, and he realized she was crying as she sang softly to herself.

Despite the bourbon, he could still taste her. A chill shot through him that had nothing to do with the icy air. He'd made her cry again because he was cold and cruel.

Gonzalez and Wainwright were forgotten, as Phillip raked his hand through the thick darkness of his hair. He was a fool to care about her. Furious at both Celeste and himself, he commanded his feelings to shut down. He always shut down before combat. It never took long. In less than five minutes, he'd no longer be human. Tears wouldn't matter. Nothing would matter except accomplishing his objectives.

He moved away from the air conditioner. Maybe it was better this way. He couldn't take another night or another day with her in his house, unless he could have her.

When she came inside, they ate dinner in silence. Oh, she tried to make conversation, and he tried to mumble appropriate answers to her idiotic questions. Why did women always want to talk when you felt like tearing furniture apart with your bare hands or ripping the oak floor up with a claw hammer?

Sweetly she asked if something was wrong with the meal.

How the hell would he know? As if he could taste anything but her. Maybe the steak—she'd actually cooked beef tonight—was delicious. Who the hell cared? He was shutting down, going deep, deep inside himself.

He was good at this game. He'd learned that if he did this before combat, the fear couldn't take over. Instead of going mad or becoming paralyzed with terror, he became inhuman and turned himself into some sort of soulless killing machine. Once, in such a state, he'd run straight at a tank in Iraq.

"We shouldn't have kissed," Celeste said.

"Wouldn't have missed it for the world," he replied.

Her glistening lashes fluttered. Somehow she seemed far away, and he was glad. Her rejection didn't hurt quite so much.

He wasn't good with rejection. The Marines had a policy—they didn't leave anybody behind. That policy was why he'd become a Marine.

He'd been left behind his whole damn life.

Rejection.

His rich socialite mother hadn't wanted him. He'd been an accident and beautiful, glamorous, Kathryn Westin's only child. He'd been a big baby, ten pounds, and she'd never forgiven him for her stretch marks. As soon as he was old enough, she'd packed him off to military school in Harlingen, Texas.

The other boys went home for the summer. He'd been sent to expensive camps near Hunt, Texas, which had an emerald-green river and was some of the most beautiful hill country in central Texas. At Christmas he'd gone to his grandmothers, who were good to him in their way. But he hadn't been close to them, and they weren't his mother. He'd rarely seen his mother. She hadn't even bothered to watch him graduate from high school or college.

Celeste stood and picked up her dinner plate, snapping him back to the present. She walked over to the sink and rinsed her dishes. Even though he knew he was in his own kitchen and she was real, not a phantom, he felt as if he was in a dream. As if she wasn't really there. As if nothing could touch him or hurt him.

"Are you okay?" she whispered, turning around when she was done.

He nodded. "Why?"

"You seem kinda strange."

"I think I'll go for a walk. Don't wait up."

As if she would—

"Oh, Phillip, Sheriff Wainwright called about that cow—"

"I know." He slammed out the door. When the light came on in the living room, he watched her settle herself on his couch to watch his television, which was something she never did, if he was in there.

Rejection. Funny, he couldn't feel a thing now.

Nobody had ever wanted him. Nobody except the Marines.

Boot camp had proved more than even he could bear, so after ten days of abusive military garbage, he'd rejected the Marines and their madmen drill instructors and had gone AWOL. He'd hidden out in the swamp that surrounded the base for a week, with nothing to eat but raw lizards and snakes, with nothing to drink but swamp water. He'd squatted up to his eyeballs in mud and scorpions and mosquitoes while platoons had searched for him. That was when he'd first learned to shut down emotionally.

The MPs had finally found him, of course, and had hauled him to the brig in handcuffs. The meanest sergeant on the base had taken over at that point. He'd made a show of verbally flaying Phillip in front of his platoon. Then he'd collared Phillip and shoved him toward his office for a private torture session. He'd pushed Phillip into a chair and slammed the door.

"A week? You ate lizards? Snakes? What were you thinking about, kid?"

"Wasn't thinking. Shut down."

"Crazy kid. You ate snakes? What the hell were you trying to prove?"

"Shut down."

The sergeant had crossed his arms over his bull-thick chest and eyeballed him. "Either you're going to make one hell of a crazy Marine. Or…"

He let that word hang like a grenade that had been thrown. His eyes narrowed. "Or I'm going to personally take you back to that swamp and feed you to the alligators and snakes myself. Do we have an understanding, kid?"

"Yes, sir."

"Do we have an understanding?" he'd screamed in that awful maniacle tone that had driven Phillip to go AWOL in the first place.

"Yes, sir!"

"Seven days on snakes and swamp water. You're a born Marine. You're crazy enough to be anything you want to be. Don't you ever forget that."

Then the sergeant had given him a fatherly pat. "Now you make me proud, son."

"Yes, sir!"

From that day, the Marines had been Phillip's home and his family. They'd been enough. Until Celeste. Now that she'd come back he wanted more.

He wanted Celeste.

Shut down! Shut down! Dive!

When he got back from his hour-long walk, Celeste was in the middle of watching some chick-flick called

When Harry Met Sally. Curled up at one end of the couch, she was munching fat-free microwave popcorn out of a sack. Her golden hair flowed down her back. Hell, she looked like an angel.

"Want some?" She smiled at him as he shut the front door and then held up her popcorn bag. When he hesitated, she shook it.

He went over to her and scooped out a handful. Their hands brushed, and to his surprise he felt a jolt.

Shut down.

Their eyes met and he felt pulled toward her like an iron filing to a powerful magnet. No matter how hard he tried to ignore her and shut down, he was failing big-time. Just the sight of her on his couch, and her golden female beauty had his blood heating and his heart pounding.

"This is a great movie," she said. "One of the best."

"Never saw it," he mumbled, determined to stumble to bed.

"'Cause you prefer those boring old war movies."

"Movies with no mush."

"Hey, sit down. Watch this! This is my favorite! Meg's in a restaurant—"

Sure enough, Meg Ryan was in a restaurant proving to Billy Crystal that a woman could fake an orgasm. Meg was cute. The scene was hot. Meg got hotter and hotter. Just watching her throw back her head and gasp made Phillip want Celeste in bed, made him want to see Celeste's face when she came.

He went around the sofa and sat beside Celeste. She squirmed a little, relocating as far from him as possible. Meg twisted and writhed and struggled to breathe. Celeste turned beet-red. She didn't look at him, though, and she didn't get up.

They pretended to watch the movie together. Every scene, every piece of dialogue between the mismatched lovers maddened him and made him want Celeste more.

Shut down! But he couldn't.

When it was over, Celeste looked as though she might cry just as she had on the porch.

"What's wrong?" Phillip whispered from his end of the sofa.

"They got together."

"It's called a happy ending. You're supposed to be happy."

She sobbed a little. "I am. I—I am."

He couldn't stand for her to cry, even over a silly movie. Used to, he would have taken her in his arms.

Don't touch her. She doesn't want you. She'll reject you.

Finally, he edged closer and took her hand in his. He fought to ignore that her fingers felt like soft, warm velvet against his rougher palm. "If they could fall in love and make it work, anybody could," he said.

What the hell are you doing, Westin?

She fell for his line—hook, line and sinker.

"Even us?" she whispered, glancing up at him with big, shy, shining eyes.

"Maybe it was too damn easy the first time," he muttered.

"Love at first sight?" she murmured on another little sob, brushing a wild strand of gold behind her ear.

"You were singing in that tight red dress. Every man in that awful bar…"

"Oh, dear, that awful dress—"

"Not awful. Sexy. So sexy."

"You came up and asked me after the fight if I needed

a ride home. You had such beautiful manners…even in that bar.''

''You wiped off my bloody brow with that napkin and said yes, so sweetly, so tenderly.''

''Yes,'' she whispered. She touched the wound on his cheek.

All of a sudden he couldn't stop looking into her big blue eyes. She had him, right where she wanted him. Or did he have her?

''No seat belt, huh?'' she whispered. ''What really happened?''

''You don't want to know.'' He pulled her closer and traced the contours of her face with his hands.

''Some silly war?''

''Can we start over?'' He wanted to know. What the hell was he doing? He was supposed to be shutting down. And here he was, coming up for air.

''You mean, sex?''

''Sex would be nice.''

''Will you hate me in the morning the way Billy Crystal—''

''I didn't run last time, did I?''

She bit her lip. ''I would've come back. You wouldn't let me.''

She would've come back. Was that true? He'd been too damned proud to go after her. ''If you run off after fame and fortune, why would you want to come back here to me?''

''Maybe they aren't enough. I wouldn't know because I never had them. I thought you'd chase me.''

''What are you really doing here? You could have gone anywhere. Why me?''

As always, that particular question made her pale and she refused to answer. And the fact that she refused to answer made him suspicious, made him want to ask that question over and over again even though he knew it made her uncomfortable.

Hell. Why was he so damn sure her coming back here to him meant something? Ego, that's why. Because he wanted to believe she'd come back to him, that was why.

If he was wrong, why had she come? If there was another reason, why wouldn't she tell him?

She leaned into him and kissed him. "You were always in my heart. You've got to believe that."

"That damn song of yours sure got to me."

"So you listened to it?"

"About a million times."

She beamed up at him.

"I've got the CD. I used to lie in bed and drink my bourbon straight from the bottle and listen to it over and over. It was as close as I could get to you."

"I wrote it for you. But I guess you figured that out."

"Yeah." He pulled her close.

"Oh, Phillip—"

To his surprise she circled his neck with her arms.

"Are you sure?" he whispered.

"You mean, about going to bed?"

He ran his hands through her hair. Even that brief contact could twist his gut into a knot. He sucked in a tight breath.

"No. But let's do it anyway," she said.

Without speaking, he carried her to his bedroom and kicked the door shut behind them.

"You can sleep in tomorrow," he murmured gently as he laid her on the bed.

"No more 0600. You're serious."

"You think so?"

"You going to leave me a list on the bedpost?"

"Make your own."

"So I've definitely won another skirmish. And the night is young. I haven't even begun."

"You have some peculiar methods, but you'd make a good combat Marine. You get your way."

"I wage my battles on the domestic front. You'd better look out. When we wake up tomorrow, this base is going to have a new commander."

"You think you're that good?"

"I know *we're* that good."

And they were. Her unsteady hands loosened his shirt buttons and unzipped his fly.

"Oh, Phillip, you smell so good…all musky and male."

When she was done and his jeans were on the floor, he undressed her.

She was as beautiful as he remembered, lush breasts, pink nipples, slim waist, and her skin smelled like flowers. He knelt in front of her and ran his hands all over her. She was like a perfect living sculpture in a museum. No art object was ever more beautiful than she. Every time he looked at her, she blushed and licked her lips. Finally, he took her in his arms and carried her to bed.

As always, this part of love was easy for them. When they touched each other, they burst into flame. Each remembered exactly what to do to give the other the most pleasure. He made love to her as slowly as he could, considering that he felt a raging need and was about to burst.

How else could he show her how much he adored her except with his hands and lips? She arched into him with a fierce passionate response that thrilled him. She clung, kissing his throat, his neck and his chest as he slowly rocked back and forth on top of her.

"Only you. Only you, Phillip," she murmured. "Only you."

"Seven years I wanted this," he said. "Why did you wait so long to come back to me?"

"Why didn't you come after me?"

No way could he tell her about one of the times he'd run away from military school to see his mother. When he'd seen the cars at the house, he'd known she was having one of her parties. She'd been so beautiful in her white sparkly dress that he'd run into her arms. She hadn't even hugged him. She'd stared at the dark stains on her white dress and said, "Your hands are dirty. Why can't you ever remember not to touch Mommy with dirty hands?" Then she'd simply picked up the phone and called the commander of his military school.

"You were the one who left," Phillip said to Celeste.

"But you didn't come..."

"I didn't know you wanted me to."

"Well, I did."

Oh, God— She kept saying that. Was it true? Did she want him? Had she wanted him even then...and...all this time he'd felt rejected?

Thrilled at these musings, he thrust into her deeply. Being inside her tight warmth was everything he'd remembered and more. She completed him as nothing else could.

Oh... This was where he belonged, inside her. He forced himself to move slowly. He wanted this to last, but she was in a hurry.

Clasping his waist, she hugged him hard. "Please... Now! Now! I can't wait!"

When it was over, they talked for hours.

* * *

The next morning Celeste opened her eyes and saw the golden sunlight streaming through the gauzy white curtains she'd hung in Phillip's bedroom. She was alone.

Mourning doves were cooing. Leaves were rustling outside. There were no traffic sounds. She smiled dreamily, hugging herself. The country quiet was so different from the neon glitter of Vegas.

Slowly after she woke up, she got up and raised the window and stuck her head out to breathe in the fresh warm air. Mission Creek wasn't so bad, not even for a girl who wanted to be a star. Not if she had Phillip.

Phillip had been so tender and sweet, so incredibly gentle, and this morning she felt like a woman deeply in love. The angst she'd felt when she'd lived with him before, her heart burning with the desire to be a star, was momentarily gone. Those past seven years had been filled with loneliness and disappointment. For now, last night with Phillip was enough. She felt a peace she'd never known before, a rightness, and a sense of belonging.

Where was he? She wanted him again. She could see her guitar where she'd left it propped outside against the back wall of the porch. It was funny. This morning she could stare at the guitar and feel nothing for it. All she wanted was Phillip to come into the bedroom and smile at her, to take her in his arms again. What did that mean?

The phone rang, jarring her out of her tranquil mood. She didn't answer it because she thought Phillip should answer it since most of the calls were for him. Even when it kept ringing, she let it. She didn't feel like talking to anybody. Then she giggled. Except maybe Phillip. He'd licked her all over. There were so many delicious things she wanted to do with him.

Finally, when the phone wouldn't stop ringing, she picked it up and said hello into the receiver.

"Baby!" Puff. Wheeze.

Alarm bells in her head went off like sirens in a fire station. "Johnny!" Cupping the phone, she lowered her voice. "You and I are through."

"But…baby—"

She turned her back to the door. "Through! *Finito!* ¡*Terminado!* Do you understand?"

"We have a contract."

"Tear it up! We are through! Do you un-der-stand? Through!"

"O-oh, no," he groaned. She heard a terrible pounding on his end.

"Johnny! That sounds like wood splintering—"

"They're at the door!" Gasp. Puff. Puff. "Call you later."

"Who's— No—don't dare call me here—"

"Catch you later, baby." He hung up.

"Johnny—" When he didn't answer she shook the phone.

Another voice said, "This is Nero. Remember me?"

She began to shake.

"You can't hide," Nero said.

"You'd better not show up here! You'd better not!" She slammed the phone down.

Oh, dear. She had to tell Phillip about this. But how could she tell Phillip? She began to pace. Phillip didn't understand about Johnny. He was jealous and hurt because Johnny had picked her up and driven her to Vegas. Would he believe her if she told him the truth? He was a Marine. Honor mattered to him.

Oh, why hadn't she been smarter? Johnny had been a disaster from start to finish. She'd been an idiot not to dump him long before now. But he'd fed her promises that had kept her dream alive.

Would Johnny tell the loan sharks where she was? Could they trace her by hitting Redial or something? Her heart plummeted. Yes, Johnny would tell. Yes, they could hit Redial. Nero had sounded pretty determined. If Johnny didn't come up with the money, there was no telling what he and The Pope would do.

She had to tell Phillip. He wanted to know why she'd left Vegas. She had to tell him. But he was so stolid and strong. He believed in lists and rules, in living by the book. He wouldn't approve of Johnny and his awful loan sharks. He wouldn't approve of Harry's, either, or of her working there.

In a scared little voice she began to sing, "Johnny, be good." And soon as she did, she felt stronger, strong enough to put Johnny's call and Nero's threat out of her mind.

Phillip's truck roared up in the drive. She had to put on something beautiful. Phillip was home. Phillip—

No sooner had she slipped into a pink cotton dress than the front door banged.

"I'm home," Phillip yelled.

"In here," she cried, tearing the dress off.

He stomped down the hall and opened the door. The pink dress lay over a chair.

"Oh, my. Still in bed?"

She fluffed her hair. "Worn out. You're too good a lover."

"Now that's a complaint a man doesn't mind hearing."

When he sat beside her, she kissed him.

"Hot kiss! Lots of tongue! What's that all about?"

She grinned. ''Just checking to see if you're in the mood.''

He stripped off his shirt. His boots hit the floor with two loud clunks.

''Looks like you're in the mood—''

''Always with you,'' he said.

Five

***

Celeste stretched lazily, curling her body against Phillip's. Oh, dear…. She felt limp and happy, completely without a care or a fear. Phillip was as hot as a furnace. Enveloped in his masculine warmth, she felt as if she was sinking into a delicious sensual spell.

"Mmm… I want to stay like this forever."

"Can I shut the windows yet?" Phillip asked, kicking at the sheet with his foot. "It's hotter than the shades of Hades."

"Poor baby," Celeste cooed without the least bit of sympathy as she twisted around playfully and dropped her gaze to the mat of black hair on his wide chest. He had the air conditioner on and she had the window open.

"Or at least turn on a fan?" he grumbled.

It was way after midnight. Awash in moonbeams, the lovers lay awake in a tangle of sheets. Wrapped in each other's arms they were satiated from lovemaking. Or at least Celeste was.

"But the fan makes so much noise we won't be able to hear the cicadas."

"The air in here is as thick and warm as hot jelly."

Phillip was exaggerating. He had the air-conditioning going full blast.

"Jelly. Yummy."

He mopped a hand across his perspiring brow.

"The window being cracked is not why you're so hot, lover buver, and you know it," she teased. "We're like a pair of spent noodles."

"Straight out of the boiling pot."

"I have no complaints." She stroked her hand through the thick matted hair of his chest, down his waist.

He laughed when she circled him down there, and the deep rumble rippled through her and made her nestle against his hot, muscular body.

"Woman, look what you did to my clam digger. It's pretty pitiful."

"What?"

He lay back on the pillow and crossed his arms under his dark head. "It's the punch line in a corny joke about a boy and girl who get shipwrecked on a deserted island. It makes the rounds every time my Marine buddies get together for beers at the Lone Star Country Club or The Saddlebag. On the third or fourth beer Mercado always has to tell it. You wouldn't appreciate it."

"Try me."

"I feel like we've been in bed a week," he said, changing the subject.

"Almost."

He frowned. "The chores are damn sure piling up.

We're running low on feed and I need to break in that new saddle and those chaps.''

"Hey...hey. You talk too much.''

"Hell, I was going to hitch a plow to my bulldozer and clear the mesquite out of the north pasture.''

"That'll wait.''

He groaned. "Maybe if it had rained, I'd agree. I've got a bunch of barely weaned calves that need to eat.''

"Six days,'' she corrected softly, her mind still on their sexual marathon. "Not a whole week.''

"And six nights. Give a guy credit for the nights.''

"You're really something,'' she murmured. "And number six isn't over yet.''

"Yeah, it is. I'm thinking about all those hungry calves and the unrecoverable feed costs plus the extra pasture leases—''

"Quit thinking about them, then.'' She smiled, her heart full of love. "We did this stay-in-bed-a-week, devour-each-other's-bodies routine when we fell in love the first time,'' she mused dreamily. "Is it love at second sight this time all over again?''

He rolled over. "If it isn't, it's a damn good substitute.''

She thought of Vegas, of Johnny and the loan sharks after them both. Terror had driven her back to Phillip. But something else might keep her here. Despite the dead cow and Johnny's call, she felt so safe, so beloved, lying here beside him. It was as if a missing piece of her life had fallen into place.

"But tomorrow, we're getting up...early,'' Phillip said. "We're going to behave ourselves, act like mature adults and go back to work...feed those calves....''

"Oh, dear. End of honeymoon.''

"You're going to clean house and I'm going to pay those bills on the spindle."

"At 0600—sharp?" She saluted. Or rather, she tried. It was an impossible maneuver since she was lying in bed so close to him.

He laughed and pulled her tighter against his chest. "You can sleep as late as you like. Hey, did I tell you that there's a dance tomorrow night at the Lone Star Country Club?"

She remembered what that waitress, Mabel, had said about his girlfriends at the club. "I—I don't fit in there. I—I don't have anything to wear. Anything elegant I mean."

"We'll have to get you something, then."

She'd been dreading something like this. What if she got out and somebody recognized her as Stella Lamour? She remembered Nero's voice on the phone and shuddered. What if word somehow got back to Nero and The Pope? What if they had spies in the neighborhood and figured out where she was and came after her?

"I really wouldn't fit in," she said.

"Of course you fit in, and I'd really like to take you," Phillip persisted.

"I'd rather go for a seventh night in bed."

"We can do that after we get back from the dance. Celeste, I really do want to celebrate our getting back together formally...with my friends."

"Isn't that what we've been doing?" she whispered. "Celebrating?"

"I don't feel too formal when we're both naked."

She laughed.

"You still have doubts, don't you?" he whispered.

"I—I know we're great in bed. That part's like a fairy tale. But what about all the rest of it?" She sighed. "Do you really think such a fairy-tale relationship can last out there in the real world?''

"I want it to. Maybe all we both have to do is decide that's what we want and work at it.''

"But— A girl like me…and a guy like you…'' Pain swelled in her chest. "You come from a wealthy family. I have no family.''

"You have me.''

"But—''

"One day at a time. You tell me what's in your heart, what you really want, and I'll try to be there for you.''

Would he? What about her dreams of being a star? Why did taking their relationship to another level scare her so much? What was she so afraid of?

"I've lost everybody I ever loved,'' she blurted.

He traced his lips across her brow. "Me, too. Only I never loved anybody the way I love you.''

"I don't want to hurt you.''

"Celeste, a drill sergeant in the Marines once told me I could be anything I wanted to be. The strange thing was, I believed him, and it's made all the difference in my life.'' He toyed with a tendril of her hair. "So—I'll give you the same advice, believe in yourself. I damn sure do.''

"You're supposed to settle down with a churchgoing girl.''

"I thought that was a dumb idea even before you came home.''

"Home,'' she whispered.

She lifted her head off the pillow and gazed down at him, unconsciously memorizing the way he looked, all sweaty and hot and virile and sexy after their lovemaking.

Home? Was she the one for him? Was he the only

man for her? If so, why was she so afraid? There was so much she hadn't come to terms with—her little-girl dreams, her big-girl dreams, the bad men chasing her and the horrible fact that by staying with Phillip and not telling him about Nero and The Pope she might be deliberately putting him in danger.

She closed her eyes and swallowed the hard lump in her throat. Going out together socially to the Lone Star Country Club would make it seem as though they were a real couple, an ordinary couple. Were they? Was it really that simple? Was she ready for that?

"All the guys will be there," he said, his deep voice hopeful.

"You mean, your Marine buddies?"

"Ricky Mercado and his brother-in-law, Luke…and several of the men who served under my command in the 14th unit."

"I remember Ricky. Talk, dark and handsome— right?"

"Tall, dark…"

"Cute."

"Believe me, he's as anxious as you to renew the acquaintance as you are. Did you two—"

"I was just teasing you. I don't know, Phillip. It seems awful soon to face your friends. We'll have to explain what I'm doing here."

"Well, think about it. I'm proud of you. I want to show you off to the guys and make them jealous as hell." He slid his hand under her nape and stroked the back of her neck with his thumb. "I'm serious, very serious about our relationship."

Her heart swelled. "Oh, Phillip." She felt warmth seep through her being at his stirring words. "But what if somebody recognizes me as Stella…'' She shuddered. ''That could ruin—''

''They won't,'' he said gruffly. ''And if they do, I'm proud of your CD, proud of the way you worked so hard to make your dream come true.''

Her heart missed a beat. *You don't know about Nero and The Pope!*

''You are?'' she whispered.

''Damn proud.''

You wouldn't be if you knew that the only reason I came here was to use you as a human shield to protect me from two killers.

She remembered the dead cow and the note. Just thinking about why she'd come here made her feel so selfish and so cowardly. He was being so sweet to her.

She bit down on her lower lip. She was using him. She owed him the truth. But the truth might spoil their fragile happiness, and she'd had so little happiness.

''Okay, I'll go, Phillip.''

Relief seemed to flow through him as he relaxed and kissed her brow. ''Can I turn on the fan now?''

She nodded. He got up and shut the windows and turned on the fan. Then he came back to bed and pulled her close. He was instantly asleep, but she lay in the dark, utterly bewildered, wondering what she should do.

This past week had been pure magic. His every rough and tender kiss had stolen her breath away, stolen her heart, too.

She loved him.

She hadn't wanted to fall in love again, and she didn't want to damage their new relationship by telling him that she was involved in any way with a pair of hoodlums like The Pope and Nero. And if they tracked her here, how would she ever convince him that Johnny had lied about her to the loan sharks, that she'd done nothing wrong?

Nothing except run to Phillip and endanger him and maybe his livestock because she'd been scared out of her wits

Phillip had said he was proud of her. Oh, how wonderful his saying that had made her feel. She wasn't ready to jeopardize Phillip's good opinion of her. Not yet. Their relationship was too new and fragile and precious.

"Do you want to dance?" Phillip whispered in Celeste's ear.

"Oh, yes!" She set her purse on the table. Anything to escape the escalating tension at their table. Her own nerves had started skittering at her first sight of the four-story clubhouse and its rolling lawns.

"Excuse us, gentlemen," Phillip said as he helped Celeste out of her chair.

She smiled at his friends brightly, maybe too brightly—her star-wattage smile. When every man in the room turned to admire her, Phillip swore under his breath.

"Do you have to be so damned sexy?"

She threw her head back and laughed.

"Minx," he said in an awed whisper.

She'd dressed up in a slinky red dress that hugged every curve. She'd put on lots of makeup and fixed her hair because she was so afraid of all the beautiful women Phillip had dated at the club.

She gripped his arm as he led her across the elegant room to the dance floor.

"Relax. You're the most beautiful woman here and the only one for me."

''Really?''

''Really, damn it.''

''Is my dress too loud?''

''You look sensational.''

She hated being so insecure. She wanted and needed him to say things like that over and over.

Lavish bouquets of long-stemmed roses of all colors decorated the tables of the Lone Star Country Club dining room. Celeste and Phillip had a candlelit table in a corner with Phillip's handsome friends from the 14th unit—Flynt Carson, the local millionaire rancher, Spence Harrison, the former D.A., Tyler Murdoch, a bomb expert, and Luke Callaghan, Ricky's brother-in-law.

Luke was wearing dark glasses because he'd been blinded by scrap metal in a mission and was only just now recovering his vision. Like Phillip, Luke trusted Ricky completely, despite the rest of the gang's doubts.

Unlike her, Phillip seemed so relaxed and at ease in his country club with his successful friends. Celeste knew he wasn't an extremely wealthy man, but he had his Marine retirement and he'd inherited. Compared to her, he was very comfortable financially.

Some of the guys were married and settled now, but this weekend their wives were away in San Antonio shopping. Ricky Mercado, the black sheep of the bunch because his family had Mafia connections, had come in late and was now slouching at the far end of the table. He'd had too many beers and his attitude was that of a sulky jungle cat. Phillip believed Ricky had gone straight, but Mercado was ready to pounce at any remark or glance the other guys made that he didn't like. Not that his attitude slowed his former guys down much.

Even though Phillip and Celeste were sitting between Mercado and the rest of the men, thereby bodily separating them, and Luke, Ricky's brother-in-law, had been hard at work to defuse the situation, the other guys knew what to say and do to irritate Mercado. Thus, Ricky's mood had worsened with each beer.

Not that Phillip seemed upset by Mercado's glowering face. Celeste, however, had wanted everybody to be happy. She'd begun feeling nervous when Mercado had started telling a story about Phillip putting his life in danger by charging three snipers. She hadn't wanted to hear about Phillip's near-death experiences so she was glad Phillip had put his hand on her waist, glad he'd led her to the dance floor.

"Quit twisting that ring 'round and round' your finger. Didn't I tell you, you're stunning?" Phillip whispered when they reached the dance floor. "Didn't all the guys say you were beautiful? Too damn many times? Even Mercado?"

"It was the only nice thing he's said. But why would you take on three snipers?"

"Mercado was exaggerating. Hey, you look good in red. You look like a star. Like Stella—"

"You clean up nice, too," she murmured as he folded her into his arms. Maybe it was best not to think about those stories when she didn't have to. "There are so many beautiful, elegant women here. Have you...dated any of them?"

He frowned. "A few."

"Quite a few?" she asked, feeling even more insecure.

He was silent for a long moment. Then he touched her hair and tilted her chin up so he could meet her troubled gaze.

"Yes." He hesitated. "None of them were you."

She rested her cheek against his chest.

"You're different, Celeste."

"You'd say that to them, too."

"Maybe. But this isn't a line. I'm telling you the truth. I don't care who you are or who you've been or who you've been with before. I don't care where you came from. I need you. Just you. I don't know why. I just do. Honey, you're so damn beautiful and so sweet…not to mention the things you think up to do in bed."

"I've got a good idea for tonight." She whispered a fantasy into his ear.

He chuckled. "Hold that thought."

"Promise you won't think I'm kinky."

"It'll only seem kinky the first time."

The music started and his powerful body moved slowly against her petite frame. As always they were a perfect fit. For a few magic moments she forgot everything but Phillip, but then she grew aware of Mercado's darkening stare. The voices from their table were growing louder.

"Ricky looks so unhappy and the guys, I mean, except for Luke—"

"Hold your head up," Phillip whispered. "Look at me. Forget Ricky and the guys. They'll work out their issues about Mercado. He told me he doesn't work for his family and I believe him. And besides, Luke's holding down the fort while we dance."

She stared so deeply into his silver eyes and forced herself to forget the tension they'd left behind at their table. He was so gorgeous, he mesmerized her. Just looking at him, even in front of all these people, she was sure she lost a piece of her soul to him forever.

"You have nothing to be ashamed of, Celeste. You are as classy as any woman here."

Would he believe that when he found out Vegas loan

sharks were hot on her trail? And what if it turned out they'd killed his cow?

Soon she forgot Nero and The Pope and the guys, and surrendered to the music. Not that Phillip and she really danced. They held each other tightly, their bodies swaying as other beautiful couples swirled around them.

Every woman seemed to cut her eyes at Phillip. Oh, dear. He was so dreamily handsome in his dark suit, dress shirt and dark tie. He didn't have an elegant body as did some of the men at the club. He was too powerfully built and hard-edged. But in his suit he could almost pass for a gentleman.

What woman wouldn't want him? Oh, why had she picked such a flashy dress? The other women were dressed far more conservatively. Next time she'd wear black…long sleeves…

If there was a next time.

"I think this is a waltz," Celeste said a little nervously because the other men weren't crushing their elegant dates and wives to their bodies as sensually as Phillip held her. She didn't want to make a spectacle of herself. "One, two, three. One, two, three…"

"I don't give a damn what kind of dance it is as long as I get to hold you," he murmured, pressing her even closer so that they were thigh to thigh.

"We could have stayed home and done this," she murmured in a shaky tone.

"Things would've gotten a whole lot wilder at home."

His arms tightened around her. She laughed, remembering how he'd caught her on the back porch last night, carried her inside and stripped her in the living room.

They swayed to the music. There was something so sexy about being fully dressed and having to restrain their passion in such a refined setting. Anybody who saw them had to know what they really wanted to do was to strip each other naked.

"The guys love you. They understand why I love you, too."

"I hope I made a good impression. I want you to be proud of me."

"Proud? They're jealous as hell. Especially Mercado."

"Why do the other guys dislike him?"

"Long story. Mercado's okay, though."

"But the other guys…"

"They'll figure out I'm right. You'll see."

The dance ended. When they went back to the table, Ricky, who looked even angrier than before, stood and jerked her chair out. "You call that a waltz, old buddy?" he muttered, attempting a light tone. "You're losing your touch." The other guys frowned at him, but he only scowled back at them.

"Relax, bro," Luke whispered.

Before she could sit, Ricky grabbed Celeste's hand. "My turn," he growled, tugging her away from Phillip. "If it's okay with you, old buddy?"

Of course, after that, all of Phillip's friends had to dance with her. Watching them from the table, Mercado grew more sullen by the minute. Then dinner was served and for a while the tensions at their table eased.

Most of the men had lobster tails with a thick buttery sauce, the kind of sauce Celeste didn't approve of. Mercado refused to eat, saying he'd drink his dinner. Phillip had ordered a slab of steak at least four-inches thick, along with a baked potato he stuffed with sour cream and chives.

When everybody was eating, Ricky said, "I'm glad

you're back, Celeste. Glad you're taming the old war-monger.''

"Warmonger?" she whispered. "He's retired from all that.''

"In your dreams,'' Mercado said.

Ty and the other Marines shot Mercado a warning look, but he ignored them and said, "Now that you're home, sir, maybe I won't receive any sudden calls to go down to Central America.''

"Central America?" Terrified, Celeste set her fork down. "What do you mean? Ricky—what on earth are you talking about?''

"Ever heard of a hellhole called Mezcaya?''

"Hell, Mercado," Luke whispered. "See what you've done, she's as pale as a sheet.''

"Mezcaya?" she whispered in alarm. "Isn't that the country in Central America that's a breeding ground for terrorists?''

"Ever heard of a particularly nasty little group called El Jefe?" Mercado asked. "They run guns...even from here in Mission Creek.''

Phillip interrupted. "Can't we talk about something else? How about the weather?''

"Has he been down to Mezcaya recently?" Celeste whispered, afraid to hear the answer.

"That cut on his cheek. Picked up some shrapnel in Mezcaya right before you showed up on his doorstep, Celeste, didn't you old buddy?''

"It was a rock," Phillip said. "A lousy rock.''

"Hell, you nearly bought it," Ricky said.

Spence hissed at Mercado to shut up, but when Phillip shot Spence a warning look, Spence stabbed his potato rather violently.

"All he told me was that he wasn't wearing a seat belt," Celeste murmured tightly.

Ricky laughed. "Why would he be wearing a belt— in The Cave?"

"The Cave?"

"Short for dungeon, sweetheart. He killed a guy, so they locked him up. Ty got him out. When the chopper came—"

"Chopper?" Suddenly her throat squeezed shut and she could barely breathe. "Phillip, you said you'd retired—"

"I am! Damn it, Mercado," Phillip began. "Celeste lost her mother and her father when she was young. She has a thing about close calls and death."

"Don't we all?" Mercado muttered. "So, I guess you didn't tell her about Mendoza or the fact you think his crazy son killed that cow on your ranch to warn you—"

"I'd appreciate it if you didn't upset her—"

"Who's Mendoza?" Celeste asked.

"Nobody. Just this murdering terrorist Westin killed."

"That's enough," Phillip thundered.

Mercado shoved back his chair. "Hey, I know where I'm not welcome."

"Finally," Tyler snapped.

"Easy," Luke said. "Why don't we talk about something else?"

"Because maybe I want to talk about what I want to talk about!" Mercado thundered. "El Jefe is right here in Mission Creek, and all of you know it. Phillip and Wainwright have the FBI looking.... Somebody gave this guy Yardley my name."

"Because of your lousy family," Tyler said.

"Cool it, both of you," Phillip's whisper was even

more deadly than his hard Marine-issue voice. "Don't make a scene. Not here."

"I had nothing to do with any cow or running guns." Ricky threw his napkin down and stood. "Sorry to eat and run."

"Eat and run?" Celeste said, swallowing the lump of fear in her throat.

"Drink and run, you mean," Spence countered.

"Please stay, Ricky," Celeste pleaded.

Luke and Phillip stood as well, and Ricky muttered something under his breath for Phillip and Luke that she could overhear.

"They keep looking at me, making digs about my family and the Mafia...setting the FBI on me.... My former friends...."

"Okay," Phillip said.

"I don't like it. I can't take it."

"Stick it out," Luke advised.

"Maybe I don't feel as comfortable around the old gang anymore as you do—sir. And you do—Luke."

"Look. Nobody said anything to Wainwright or the FBI. You severed your ties with the Mafia," Phillip said.

"Nobody but you and Luke buys that line."

"They will if you hang in there," Phillip said. "Quit drinking. Order dinner."

"Sorry, sir." Ricky leaned down and lightly kissed Celeste's cheek. "Keep up the good work, pretty lady. This *old* rascal is going to take a lot of taming."

Mercado turned on his heel and strode abruptly through the dancing couples, breaking several apart before he made it out the door.

"Good riddance," Spence said.

When Harrison made an obscene gesture, Luke and Phillip gave him warning looks.

"Forget Mercado. All we have to do is get rid of you, old man, and we'll have her all to ourselves," Tyler kidded, attempting to ease the tension.

"Sir," Phillip said.

Ty laughed. "Sir."

"No chance would I leave her with you all," Phillip said, relaxing.

"Any chance of wedding bells?" Spence wanted to know.

Celeste blushed, but she felt relieved now that Mercado had gone and the mood had lightened up.

"How'd the two of you meet?" Luke and Flynt asked in unison.

"She was singing a love song."

They all hooted.

"Well, if she can sing to you, she can damn sure sing to us," Luke said.

One by one, they demanded that she sing to them.

She turned questioningly to Phillip. "I don't think…"

But Ty was on stage with the mike. "We have a star in our midst." Phillip's buddies started clapping and cheering.

"We're outnumbered, honey," Phillip said. "Go on. Let's don't make a scene."

Slowly, she got up and Phillip led her to Ty, who held the mike. Phillip gave the bandleader a big tip, and she told them what to play. Celeste, a natural star, brought the house down when she sang her one big hit. Then she surprised Phillip and sang a song she'd just written called "Lone Star Love Song."

When the last plaintive syllable died, the crowded ballroom was silent. Then everybody started clapping and whistling and screaming for more.

"More… More…" The guys began to stomp.

"Thank you, everybody," she murmured. With a shy blush and a graceful little bow, she demurred, and Phillip led her back to their table.

"You're good. You remind me of somebody I've heard or seen before," Spence said, a frown on his handsome face.

"She's a natural star," Phillip agreed. "Honey, you were the hit of the gathering."

She blushed nervously again with even more glowing pleasure because Phillip was praising her singing, and he was proud of her.

"I know that song," Luke said. "'Nobody but you....' I used to play it all the time. Reminded me of this girl who dumped me. Who sang it? Who wrote it? Stacy? No..."

"I don't know," she lied, squeezing Phillip's hand so he wouldn't give her away.

Spence and Luke said they had to go. Just as their party was beginning to break up, two men entered the ballroom. One was a wide-shouldered hunk whose grim, hard-edged face brought butterflies to Celeste's stomach.

Oh, dear. The man was tall and trim with thick brown hair.

Vegas. Harry's. "Not Cole Yardley," she whispered. "Don't let it be..."

It was.

"What?" Phillip demanded, eyeing her first and then the two newcomers at the door. "Do you know the sheriff?"

"The sheriff?" She began to fidget with her napkin. "I—I've listened to a few of his messages. I—I think I need to go to the ladies' room."

"You just went. Do you know Justin Wainwright or not?"

The sheriff waved and Phillip waved back to him.

Cole Yardley shot her a dark glance.

She lowered her eyes. Oh, dear. This was bad. Cole Yardley was here in Mission Creek with the sheriff, and he remembered her.

If he could find her, anybody could. Oh, dear. What if he said something about that awful night in Harry's to Phillip?

"Can we go home?" she whispered, frantic when Yardley and the sheriff ambled toward their table.

"Not until I find out what Wainwright and the guy who frowned at you wants."

"He did not frown at me."

"Well, he damn sure wasn't looking at me."

If only Cole Yardley would quit glowering at her.

"You know him, don't you?"

"N-no," she said.

The sheriff joined them. "Sorry to interrupt a social gathering, but Yardley here just rolled into town."

Phillip nodded. Everybody introduced himself.

"Glad to meet you, *Celeste*," Yardley said tersely.

"Glad to meet you, Mr. Yardley," she said.

Silently she begged him not to give her away.

"Yardley here is a federal investigator," Justin Wainwright said. Justin handed Cole Yardley's business card to Phillip. "He's here about your dead cow and your suspicions about that arms-dealing ring. Like you, he suspects El Jefe may be operating in our area."

"In Mission Creek?" Celeste blurted.

"Just listen to what he has to say," Wainwright said.

"I admire your work, Westin. I know you've fought for years to bring down El Jefe." Yardley glanced at Celeste when she began to bite her lip.

"Who's El Jefe?" Celeste whispered. "I forget."

"Not who. What! El Jefe is the biggest terrorist ring in Mezcaya."

"Right. Which is in Central America," Celeste said.

"We were just discussing this," Phillip offered.

Yardley cocked his brows, but Phillip didn't embellish.

Mezcaya again. "We were just leaving," Celeste said. The talk about Mezcaya was making her nervous. Phillip had nearly died in Mezcaya right before she'd come. She didn't really want to know about Phillip being involved with terrorists. A second worry was that at any moment Yardley might decide to tell everybody how he and she had met in Vegas.

Phillip had said he was retired. While the men talked, she found herself staring at the red mark on his cheek. She didn't care about the dead cow or El Jefe. She had so many vital questions and they were all personal. Was Phillip capable of settling down even if he loved her? Was she capable of giving up her music for him? Did she even want to? Were they as mismatched as ever? Did people like them settle down? Or did they need a rush other people could live without?

The applause tonight had thrilled her. Still, more than the applause, the gleam of pride in Phillip's eyes when she'd sung had warmed her heart. But was his love enough?

"I believe your friend, Mercado, is still involved in the Mafia," Yardley was saying. "And running guns."

First Mezcaya. Now the Mafia. What was Phillip involved in?

"No way," Phillip countered.

"He just may be the ringleader of this nasty, little weapons-smuggling operation I'm investigating."

"You'll never convince me of that," Phillip said in his flat, Marine-issue voice.

"He was just down in Mezcaya."

"You want to know why? To help Ty Murdoch save my ass. I was slated for execution and he was part of the rescue team."

"Execution!" Celeste gasped. The truth at last!

Phillip had nearly died—again. And he hadn't told her. "Oh, dear. Oh, dear."

"If he wasn't involved with those bastards, how'd he know you were in trouble?" Yardley asked. "Then as soon as you and…and this young lady get back here, somebody kills your cow and leaves you a note."

"You're grilling me but you're looking at my girl. You two know each other or something?"

Yardley and she shook their heads, but neither of them could meet Phillip's gaze.

"Where are you from, anyway, Yardley?" Phillip demanded in a voice charged with both annoyance and jealousy.

Yardley glanced at Celeste.

Phillip skimmed Yardley's business card. "Your card says your office is in Vegas."

"We don't know each other," Celeste whispered, but she blushed hotly.

Phillip stared at Yardley.

"I never saw her before in my life. And believe me, I would remember a face like hers."

"She's a hard woman to forget," Phillip said stiffly. "Well, it's late. I'm tired." He stood.

"If you hear anything, anything at all that's the least bit suspicious, give me a call," Yardley said. "If you lose any more livestock…"

"Sure." Phillip's voice and manner were curt.

When Celeste and Phillip were in his truck, Phillip said, "You never did tell me why you abandoned your career in Las Vegas and came here in such a hurry. Did something happen? Was Yardley your lover?"

"I can't believe…" she whispered. "How could you ask me such a thing?"

"Fasten your seat belt," he muttered. Then he stomped down hard on the accelerator.

She gave a little cry when the truck shot forward into the darkness. Soon the silence inside the cab was so thick between them Celeste hardly dared to breathe.

She stared out the window. He watched the yellow lines in the center of the road fly past.

When they got home, she got out of the truck and ran to the front stairs, only to stumble over something warm and sticky. When she fell forward, black eye sockets stared up at her.

She screamed, and Phillip flew to her when she convulsed in tears and pulled her off the bloated object.

"I—it's a dead…cow," she sobbed. "A-another one. On…on the first step…"

"It's okay."

"There's another note—"

Phillip ripped off the note somebody had nailed to the porch railing.

"'You hurt my family, so now I will hurt yours,'" Phillip read.

"Another cow," she whispered. "Two cows. Why would anybody be killing your cows? I thought Sheriff Wainwright—"

"He's investigating. So am I," Phillip said.

"Is this happening because you killed that bad guy in Mezcaya and didn't tell me about it?"

"I don't know, damn it. With your kind of logic, I

could blame you. Cows didn't start dying till you came here.''

''Oh?'' She felt a rush of guilt and fought to cover it. ''Sure! Blame me!'' She turned away, so he couldn't read her face.

''I was making a point.''

''This is about you, not me! What are you doing behind *my* back?''

''What are you doing behind mine, Celeste? You're not telling me where you're coming from, either.''

''Are you about to go off on a mission again and get yourself killed the next time?''

''You're hiding something, too, Celeste. What the hell is going on? Are you going to run off with Yardley or something?''

''What?''

''Did he come here because of you? Is he your next Johnny Silvers?''

''D-don't be ridiculous. He's investigating your gun smugglers!''

''*My* gun smugglers? Hell!'' He stared at her.

''I'm tired,'' she said. ''And I'm going to bed. To my old room down the hall. Thank you for a *lovely* evening.''

''My pleasure.'' His tone was hard—pure Marine issue. ''I'll call the sheriff and then get rid of the cow.''

She picked up her skirt and walked carefully around him and the mutilated cow. He raced up the stairs and unlocked the door for her. It was hours before the sheriff came and finished his business, hours before Phillip and Juan finished dealing with the dead cow and Phillip finally stomped up the stairs and came inside.

She was still awake, lying in her bed at the end of the hall, staring up at the spidery threads of moonlight on the ceiling. When she heard his heavy tread in the hall, she ached to run into his arms. Instead, she buried her face in her pillow.

His door opened and closed, and he went to bed alone, just as she had.

She hugged herself as she had so many times when she'd lain awake in the dark after her mother had died. Every time she closed her eyes, she saw black eye sockets. She wanted Phillip's arms around her so badly, it was all she could do not to get up and run down the hall to his bed.

Would she always always be that grief-stricken little girl who cried too easily because she was starved for true love?

Six

The honeymoon was over. After a sleepless night worrying about Yardley, and being scared about the second dead cow, and sick that she and Phillip had quarreled, Celeste got up in the dark several hours before 0600. It upset her that Phillip, Mr. Big Macho Marine, could sleep like a baby even when she ran the vacuum down the hall.

She didn't hear a peep from his bedroom until well after ten. When she finally heard him in the shower, she was on the way to the utility room, her arms aching under the weight of a third, huge load of laundry.

There was a lot of dirt on a ranch, at least in dry south Texas. When Phillip came in from a hard day's work in some distant pasture, his carved face would be streaked with mud because he'd perspired so much that the blowing dust had stuck to him. His clothes and hair would be caked with grit. The dirt seeped under doors and through cracks and crannies of the window frames. Dusting had to be done every single day.

That gloomy morning after the dance, Celeste made herself two pots of coffee. Wired from so much caffeine and exhausted from no sleep and the hours of house-work, the blissful six days of their marathon lovemaking in Phillip's bed seemed like a long-ago dream. So did her ambition to be a star.

Maybe it was for the best that Mercado, Yardley, rumors about dangerous gunrunners, and the dead cow had turned up to burst her little romantic bubble. Phillip and she were as different as two people could be. Maybe she lusted after him and ached for his sweet smiles and praise. Maybe they really did love each other in their way, but how long could passion alone sustain them? Her failures in the music world had taught her that making it in the real world was an everyday matter. So was love and marriage.

She didn't want to be married to a soldier who left her and went off to war while she stayed home to panic at every phone call because she was so afraid somebody would phone to say he was dead and she'd lose everything again. And did he want a girl who couldn't give up her impractical dreams of being a country-western star?

Mercado had him figured. In between adventures like chasing gunrunners, Phillip needed some nice society, church girl, one of those rich, proper beauties from the country club who dressed like a lady. Someone who was content to be a stay-at-home wife while he was gone.

Celeste was different. She had a voice and a need to be more than she was. Only when she sang did she lose the awful feeling that she was an invisible little nothing. If she dressed flashy and sang her heart out, it was because she craved attention and love. A girl didn't just have talent. Talent had the girl.

When she'd been a kid, all the other kids had had real mothers and daddies to go home to. All she'd had was her music. Singing and writing songs gave her a release from pain and a way to express herself that nothing else did. If she gave all that up for Phillip now, and he kept fooling around with gunrunners and went off again on some dangerous mission and got himself killed, where would she be—too old to make her big dream come true.

If Phillip died, she'd be a nothing. For all the fireworks and tenderness, Phillip might leave her. Her music was the only real anchor she'd ever had.

She was thirty-two. Her shot at the big time was running out. Every spare moment she got, she'd better work on her music. She had greatness in her. She knew she did. This time she'd go to Nashville.

For the rest of that week Celeste kept to her bedroom in the evenings when Phillip came in from work, and Phillip kept to his. She would cook early and leave the food on the stove. They would eat dinner at different times and avoid speaking to each other whenever possible. Even though she was curious about the dead cow, she hadn't asked him what he'd done with it or what he'd said to the sheriff or maybe to Cole Yardley. She knew Phillip was investigating the incident, but she didn't probe for details because the whole thing upset her too much.

At night Phillip went for long walks and watched television. She read and wrote and taped songs in her room. Every chance she got to go into town, she mailed a tape and a letter to Greg Furman, the producer in Nashville, who still hadn't written her back. Phillip seemed too preoccupied to notice that she'd asked for the truck more often.

At night when she was too tired to sing another note, she would crawl into her bed and curl up, lying rigidly in a fetal position, listening to the boards creak and the wind moan in the eaves. After lying in Phillip's arms and enjoying all that soul-stirring sex, it was all the harder to sleep alone without his muscular arms holding her close.

Since Phillip was an ex-Marine, he probably found it easier to stick to his sulk and content himself with investigating his mystery than she did. For him it was second nature to draw lines in the sand and then stay on his side waiting for her to surrender. Well, she wouldn't surrender. She wouldn't.

According to Wainwright and Yardley, Mendoza's men were definitely in the area. Not that Celeste invited Phillip to share his concern on that subject with her. Hell, she was barely civil.

When Phillip stalked into the house late one scorching afternoon intending to bar himself in his bedroom until it was time for dinner, the sound of Celeste's lilting voice in the bathtub brought him to an abrupt halt outside her door. Damn it. She sang those sweet, sad songs every night in her room, probably just to get to him.

The last week had been pure hell. Besides worrying about her safety, it was impossible to live with her, to hear her pour her heart out in those songs, to watch her glide from room to room, without wanting her. Everything she did was sexy, everything she wore—those tight short shorts that revealed her long legs, those skimpy T-shirts that clung to her breasts, the way her yellow hair flowed messily around her shoulders, her dreamy expression when she stared out the window. Did she yearn for bright lights, the stage, fame, and a man who could give her or at least promise her those things?

Every night he'd lain in bed thinking about her, remembering her every smile, smiles that died the minute he entered a room. She'd been driving into town a lot. Why? To flirt with other men? Cole Yardley? To plan her next escape? What did she want, really?

Why couldn't he forget how hot she'd been in his bed before their quarrel, how she'd opened her mouth and given him endless tongue, how she'd stripped and danced for him on the kitchen table? He'd shoved the dishes on the floor, and they'd done it on that table, then in the shower, on the burgundy couch, against the front door, and even in the cab of his pickup before he'd driven into town one morning.

Boots clomping, he stalked noisily down the hall, pausing at her bedroom door, only to gasp when it groaned. Had he touched it by mistake?

Instinctively he grabbed the knob, and the damned door, which had been slightly ajar, opened as if by itself. She was in the tub, splashing water and singing too loudly to notice him. He could see her plain as day.

Beyond her rumpled bed, the path to the bathroom was littered with her clothes and jewelry—those incredible short shorts, her lacy black bra and panties, that little silver chain that disappeared into her T-shirt and hung between her breasts.

Her breasts. His gaze feasted on the lush mounds. She held up a wet rag and squeezed water onto them as she sang some husky melody that he heard all the way to his bones.

It took him a while to catch his breath. She was lying back in her tub sponging her breasts with that damned pink washrag until her nipples peaked like ripe raspberries. His heart knocked violently and he went statue-still. A second glance and he felt as if he'd been slammed in the groin. Instantly he was as hard as a rock.

"I'm just a lonesome girl/lost in the middle of nowhere," she sang. "A lonesome girl in love with a lonesome man…"

But when she squeezed the water out of her rag and folded it neatly on the side of the tub, he knew he should go. She stood up, water dripping off her sleek, dewy body. Oh, God. More than anything he wanted to shove the door open and rush inside to her. But what would she do? She'd barely spoken since she'd stumbled over the dead cow.

His heart thrummed madly in his throat. Soap bubbles clung to her voluptuous, pink body as she reached for a towel. Even from the hall, he could almost smell the rose soap she used, almost taste the warm steamy water that beaded on her skin.

His gaze slid up and down her body, lingering on her breasts and then on that golden triangle of hair lower down. She'd cost him his peace of mind, his very sanity. He didn't know how to win her, but losing her wasn't an option. His objectives weren't clear. He couldn't focus on anything but her.

Oh, man. His physical reaction bothered him. He was a Marine. Where was his iron will, his disciplined Marine Corps brain? Why was it so hard to be tough with her?

Damn it. Xavier Gonzalez and the dead cows didn't bother Phillip nearly as much as his fears of losing Celeste. It took all his control not to rush inside, fall on his knees and beg her forgiveness for being so cold the past week. Fire raced through his veins. Desire had him shaking. Oh, God, she made him weak.

Why had she left Vegas? He'd called Yardley at his motel and asked him the same question. All Yardley had said in that grim voice of his was, ''Why don't you ask her?''

The man knew something; that was obvious. Had they gone to bed? Was she in some kind of serious trouble? Damn it, Phillip thought, if Celeste loved him, if she trusted him at all, she would tell him. But she didn't, and he'd been damned before he cut her any slack just because she made him feel so needy.

Somehow even with lust racing through his veins and making him crazy with uncontrollable need, he pivoted and dashed out to the barn to check on his new bulls. And he stayed there until all the lights in the house went out and he knew she was in bed. Then he came inside and called the sheriff. Wainwright and Yardley were still clueless about the dead livestock and the gunrunning activity in the area.

Celeste had the seat of Phillip's big blue pickup jammed as far forward as possible. In spite of her ongoing sulk or feud or whatever you called it with Phillip, she was radiant with excitement this morning as she started the ignition. No more cows had died mysteriously, so her fears regarding the cows had lessened.

''Lonesome Lover'' was the best song she'd taped so far. She was proud of it and anxious to get it in the mail. She was sure that this time Mr. Furman would write back.

What did Mr. Greg Furman do with her tapes anyway? Did he listen to them? Or did some secretary simply throw them in the trash? She couldn't bear that last thought.

Phillip and Juan were in the holding pens making sure all their equipment was ready for the big branding next week. Hopefully, she'd make it to town and back before either of them even noticed. But as she backed out of the garage, Phillip stalked up the drive and caught her. His Stetson was off, and he was wiping his mud-caked brow on his soft, blue chambray shirt. When he looked up, his silver eyes drilled her.

His mouth tightened. Then he waved her over. Oh, dear. Her stomach clenched. Not that bossy look. When he frowned, a prickle of alarm skidded up her spine. After barely speaking for days, he suddenly wanted to talk to her! Not good. Quickly she stuffed the incriminating envelope with her new tape in it underneath her seat.

"Hi," she said, rolling down her window as she drove closer to him. "Do you need something from town?"

"Why the hell are you going to town—again?" He leaned on her door, deliberating brushing her hand with his arm.

She jerked her hand inside. "Grocery store."

"But you went this morning."

"Oh… I—I…er, I forgot an ingredient…er, cream."

"Cream?" His gorgeous mouth smiled.

Idiot! Why did you say cream? You never cook with cream!

"My recipe needs cream," she fibbed.

His gaze slid from her scarlet face to the slim silver chain that disappeared between her breasts. "Can I come, too?"

"Aren't you busy getting ready to brand—"

"Juan knows what he's doing."

No! No! No! You can't come! Not today!

"Mind if I drive?" he whispered, opening the door.

The envelope was under the driver's side!

"Sure," she said, her voice casual as she scooted across the seat. "Go ahead. But I'd think you had better things to do."

He climbed inside, and she stared woodenly out the window. As usual the thick silence in the cab soon bristled with her doubts and his edgy hostility. She turned on the radio, the better to ignore him. The first song was about a love-'em-and-leave-'em gal. He opened his window. When he stomped on the accelerator, she leaned over and studied the speedometer. When he slowed down, she stared ahead, her eyes dazed, unfocused.

Were they going to stay mad at each other forever?

"I got an interesting phone call last night when you were at the store." His lazy drawl held an edge of menace that made her nervy with alarm.

"The sheriff? About those old cows?"

"No. Somebody else." He eyed her.

"Oh, really?" she murmured. "Anybody I know?"

"Yeah. Johnny Silver."

"I hope you hung up on him!"

"Well, I didn't."

She swallowed.

He gripped the wheel. She started to say something and then broke off, staring unseeingly ahead. Her chest felt tight.

For a few minutes the only sound in the cab was the plaintive tune about a woman loving the wrong man.

Phillip turned the volume down. "I asked him why you left Vegas in such a hurry."

She gasped and then swallowed. "You had no right—"

"I love you, Celeste." He said it so angrily, the words scared her. "Don't worry. He didn't tell me. The bastard hung up on me."

She sighed in relief.

"So, why won't you tell me why you left? Why you came here?"

"Here we go again. I was in trouble, okay? I did the smart thing and left."

He shot her a contemptuous look. "Can you be more specific?"

"It's all over now."

"All over? So why did the bastard call you?"

"So why does it matter so much to you?"

"Maybe because you matter to me." He paused. "Your friend, or whatever he is, sounded scared. I want to know why. Are you in danger?"

"Why don't you worry about your cows and gunrunners?"

"Are you in danger?"

"No," she lied. "I fired him, okay? And he's the last thing from a friend. I was young and trusting and naive in a word—stupid. He's a snake and a con artist and an out-of-control gambler. He used me. He was no good."

"I'm glad you figured that one out."

"Can we talk about something besides that human rat who can't resist a pair of hot dice?"

"Like what?"

"Like those dead cows and what happened in Mezcaya?"

"Maybe I didn't want to worry you."

"Maybe I don't want to worry you, either," she said softly.

"That's different. I don't need protecting."

"Always, always Mr. Big, Tough Hero? Get real, Phillip. Mercado said you nearly died in Mezcaya. You're human, you know. Bullets don't bounce off you any more than they bounced off those two dead cows of yours." She paused. "I know what it's like to lose some-one—"

"And you think I don't—" Phillip snapped. He sucked in a savage breath. "Your friend—I mean, the human rat sounded scared. Real scared."

"Whatever it is, it's his problem."

Phillip rolled up his window and turned off the radio. "Is it?"

She bit her lip and swallowed. "I'm not going to discuss this…until I'm ready."

"When will that be?"

"I don't know, okay?"

He sighed. "Okay."

They drove in silence for a while. Her muscles felt so tense, she ached all over.

It was one of those perfect summer mornings in south Texas. The big sky was blue and so bright she couldn't look at it without blinking, but the heat made everything hazy around the edges, especially at the horizon. A buck and a doe sprang across the road. The southeasterly breezes were playing in the oak and mesquite. Pastures stretched endlessly.

It was such wide-open country that it made their quarrel seem small and insignificant. Gradually, she began to relax.

At exactly the same moment they turned, their eyes locking on each other's faces.

"I—I…"

They both spoke in unison.

"It's beautiful out here," she said.

"Yes."

Before she thought, she smiled at him. To her surprise, his expression softened. When his gaze fell to her lips, her heartbeat came to a shattering halt.

"I've been pretty awful to you this past week," he said, leaning closer.

"Watch the road," she whispered.

"I'm sorry, Celeste."

"An apology?" Another awkward stillness descended upon both of them. "I—I can't believe I'm hearing this."

When his eyes seared her face, she felt an even greater connection.

"Neither the hell can I. Do you have any idea what surrendering costs me?"

She sighed deeply. She knew that tone. A jolt of sheer excitement lit every nerve in her body. Her heart drummed in her ears.

He concentrated on the road again.

"I'm sorry, too," she finally admitted in a rush of elation.

"I've gotta pull over, woman," he growled.

He swerved to a standstill under the deep dark shade of a spreading live oak. He took his time shutting off the engine. As his brown hand fiddled with the ignition, Celeste thought she'd never been so aware of a man.

"You found the only shady place for miles," she said.

"I want to drive home and strip you naked."

A foolish tingle shivered down her spine. The last of her self-control dissolved. "I've got an even sexier idea—"

"If it's better than mine, I can't wait to hear it."

She darted a quick, shy glance at him. When she whispered it in his ear, he laughed. In that instant their quar-

rel was over. Even before the whorls of dust settled on
the cacti and huisache, even before he unfastened her
seat belt and pulled her into his lap, it was as if she had
slipped out of her skin and into his and they were already
one.

His gaze both tender and fierce, he stared at her face
silently until everything inside her went still. She ran a
fingertip down the length of his aquiline nose. Then she
pushed a lock of dark hair from his dirty brow. All she
could hear was his breath coming quick and rasping and
her own heart beating like a savage tattoo.

"You shouldn't work so hard," she whispered.

When she moved, his eyes fell to her nipples that
thrust against her T-shirt.

A little clock on the dash ticked. The sunlight shone
on his carved cheek and black lashes. He was beautiful,
hard, masculine and dangerously virile. And he was hers,
all hers.

No…

"You have sissy eyelashes," she whispered as he
grinned and brushed his calloused fingers through her
hair.

"You're not the first girl to say that, so don't get
yourself all conceited."

"Trying to make me jealous?"

He chuckled. "I'll make it up to you later." Then he
batted his long lashes at her.

A jolt of desire swept through her. Catching her
breath, she wrapped her arms around his neck and
pressed her cheek to his. "Oh, Phillip—"

The week of doing without made it impossible for a
girl with her raging hormones to play hard to get. Even
before he kissed her, even before he drove home and

stripped her, she could already smell and taste the sex that was to come. She couldn't wait.

He tongued her lower lip and every nerve ending in her body caught fire. She melted into him.

He laughed. He knew her that well. He knew her every thought and base desire and reveled in them.

"No goody-goody church girl for me," he whispered eagerly, his eyes darkening.

A slow flush heated her cheeks, and he grinned.

"Oh, dear, you're so gorgeous," she said too breathlessly.

"So are you."

"What do you say we do something about these warm feelings—"

She hugged him. He felt so good, so warm and hard and muscular. And she felt so safe and adored.

A great tenderness welled in her heart as her soul rushed to his. Oh, dear. Not even her music was this essential. It was scary to surrender who she was to anybody, even to Phillip, even in the name of love.

"Do you want to go back to the house or do you want to do it here?" she whispered. "I can't wait much longer."

"A church girl wouldn't say that unless all the lights were out."

She cleared her throat and began to unbutton his shirt.

"I'll start the truck," he rasped thickly when she got to the third button.

"Scared you, didn't I?" she giggled. "You thought I'd really do it out here on the highway, didn't you?"

He laughed. "Wouldn't you?"

It was her turn to laugh. No sooner were they home and inside the front door, than he locked it and started to strip her. When they were both naked, she flung herself into his arms, jumped up, and circled his waist with her legs. He caught her and strutted around the house like a triumphant warrior striding home with his booty.

They never made it to the bedroom. In the hall he sank with her to the floor and kissed her, every part of her, his tongue filling her mouth and then her navel and other moist, intimate places, too, while his hands roamed. She lay still and let him do as he pleased.

When he was done he buried himself to the hilt. Then his huge, muscular body was rising and falling, carrying her with him to heights she'd never glimpsed, never dreamed were possible, and then both of them surrendered to an utter animal wildness that had her sobbing and shaking long after it was over. All the loneliness of their lives dissolved in the blistering explosions that came too quickly and yet seemed to go on and on. In the glorious aftermath she felt bathed in his love and secure; secure, and safe for the first time in her life. She was so happy, she began to cry, but he kissed away her tears and said things to make her laugh.

Afterward, when he helped her up and led her to his bed, he made time for gentle touches and tender words, but she knew that it was the shattering violence in the hall more than her tears or the sweetness in his bed that had wedded her soul to his.

Always, always she would be his no matter how she might dream of other roads to travel, no matter how much she might wish to deny it when her music carried her far away.

Seven

Phillip bathed Celeste's face, which was still hot and flushed from their lovemaking. Squeezing out the sponge, he dribbled it over her breasts and golden hair. She was reclining in the bathtub which was ringed with dozens of low candles she'd lit to give the room a warm, cozy glow. She looked so beautiful, he could have stared at her forever.

"Who are you? Who are you running from?" he murmured, setting the sponge down on the side of the tub.

There was a long silence as she stared into the flickering glow of the candles.

She took a deep breath. "I can't even walk much less run."

He encircled her wrists with his big brown hands. "Will you stay here forever...with me?"

As he gazed into her eyes, the pulse in her throat ticked nervously. "Does my answer matter to you so much? We have this moment. Now. It seems scary to pin everything down Marine-fashion.''

Marine-fashion? What the hell did she mean by that? It required immense control to keep his voice level. He was used to being in charge, to mapping out strategies and seeing them through. Her temperament was more whimsical and artistic. It was the best thing and the worst thing about her.

"What about marriage…children?" he asked.

"I never had a real home. I can't imagine what all that would be like or if I'd be capable of being a good wife and mother.''

"Frankly, I don't know much about happy homes or happy marriages, either. We'd have to take it a day at a time, make it happen. We could do it, Celeste. I know we could…but we've got to try.''

"You want this perfect housewife.''

"I used to think so." He gazed at her. "You've taught me a lot about what I want.''

"Ready for another lesson in love, Mr. Big, Tough Marine?" Her voice was soft and a little breathless.

He knew the conversation was making her uncomfortable, so she was seducing him. He should stop her. But it didn't matter what his logical mind knew. A few flicks of her talented fingertips drifting down the flat plain of his stomach and then stroking between his legs was all it took to unleash a floodtide of desire. A few teasing kisses in all the right places had him groaning out loud and begging for more. A few more kisses with a lot of tongue had him grabbing her by the waist and hauling her out of the tub to his bed.

Her skin was steamy warm from the tub, her breath soft and uneven as she lay beneath him, her golden hair fanning out upon the pillows.

"You smell like roses," he growled.

"But I'm all wet. We should get a towel or something."

"Let me look at you."

For a long moment he reveled in her lush, opulent beauty, in her utter femininity. Dark, pointy nipples. Legs that went forever.

"You don't need makeup or flashy dresses. You're a natural beauty."

"You look pretty good yourself—brown, hunky, big."

He grinned. "Big—my favorite compliment."

She'd changed his whole world and in such a short time. Even his room wasn't his anymore. She'd placed flowers and colorful pillows and pictures in every room. There were cumbersome, useless little knickknacks on every flat surface, pictures where once there had been blank spaces on his walls. She'd been here a mere month and already his ranch house felt like home instead of some bachelor's military boot camp.

Damn it. He wanted her. He wanted her here forever. But she had a point. What they had together would do...for now.

Desire burned through him, destroying every well-thought-out plan he had ever made. No perfect, well-bred, society, churchgoing woman, a woman anxious to have a man's ring on her finger and the security of marriage for him. He wanted Celeste—wild, artistic, whimsical, unrealistic Celeste. He wanted whoever or whatever she was. He wanted all of her, every part of her. And every time he had her in bed only made him want her more.

"Honey, you consume me."

"Just love me," she whispered. "I can't get enough of you, either."

For now, he thought grimly. But, at least, he had her for now.

Mabel winked at Phillip as she set his second mug of coffee on the counter. Not that he was in the mood for her chatty attentions today. She was in between husbands, and she liked to gossip and flirt with any man who showed up at the café.

He stirred his coffee and yawned, trying to look bored.

Mabel wasn't fooled. "Missed you," she said, leaning on the counter beside him to show off her ample curves. "You haven't been in to flirt much lately."

"Missed you, too," he replied dryly, but he kept stirring his coffee.

"I nearly called you yesterday," she said.

"Why?"

When he looked up, she smiled slyly and ran a fingertip through her brown curls. "A pair of sleazes came in here asking about that greasy-haired sexpot with the guitar that came here in that ripped, black cocktail dress…. You know…the girl you hired as your maid."

"You don't say." His voice cut like dry ice. "She still around?"

Mabel knew she was. The whole town knew. She was just fishing for more details, so she could feed the gossip mill.

"What'd you tell 'em?"

"That I never seen nobody like her in my café."

"Thanks."

"Bad-looking pair, if you ask me. Slick and mean. Both of them have snakes' eyes. What'd she do—kill somebody? She's on the run, that's for sure. You'd better be careful.''

He thought about his dead, mutilated cattle. Xavier was after him. But who the hell was after her?

''What did they look like?''

''One's dark, and the other is sick and pasty-faced-looking. Oh, and he wears glasses. And they both have cruel, black eyes.''

''Their eyes obviously made an impression.''

She lifted a brow. ''Y'all be careful out there, you here— If I were you, I'd strap on a gun when I left the house—''

''Thanks.''

Phillip finished the last of his coffee. Then he gave her a big smile and a tip that made her smile even bigger. Not that Phillip was smiling when he climbed in his truck.

What'd she do—kill somebody?

Phillip remembered Mendoza sailing off that jungle mountain road. Phillip knew what he'd done, but what the hell had she done?

Instead of going to the feed store as he'd planned, he stepped on the gas and rushed home to make sure Celeste was okay. It didn't take a genius to figure out those jerks had to be the reason she'd left Vegas. Phillip remembered Johnny Silver's frightened voice. The guy had panted between every word. He was up to his eyeballs in whatever this was, too. She said she wasn't involved with Silver, but she was.

She'd lied.

Why?

Damn it. She had to tell him what was going on— now. Today. Period.

But he never had the chance to ask her what had gone

down in Vegas because when he roared up to the porch, she ran out of his house in blood-splattered clothes. Tears streamed down her cheeks as she hurled herself into his arms before he could even climb the first stair.

"A-another cow," she gasped brokenly. "Only whoever it was chopped the cow in several pieces in the corral. I—I tripped over…over a leg before I saw… Then I slipped in a pool of blood. Oh, it's all too awful… I—I found this—" She was holding a bloody piece of crumpled paper.

He ripped it out of her trembling hand.

"Oh, Phillip— The…the note's like the others."

He read it out loud. "'You hurt my family, so now I will hurt yours.'"

Celeste shuddered against him. She was so small and petite, so defenseless, really.

Snakes' eyes…? Mabel had said. *What'd she do—kill somebody?*

He pressed her closer. He didn't care what she'd done. If anybody so much as laid a finger on one shiny, golden hair, he'd kill them as coldly and as ruthlessly as he'd run Mendoza off the road.

"Oh, Phillip, I—I thought you were never coming home. I called your cell—"

"It's okay," he whispered, stroking her hair as she shuddered against his chest. "Hey, hey. I was in a no-service area for a while, that's all."

"Does this have something to do with that El Jefe terrorist group?"

"Don't you worry about it. I'll handle it."

He'd better. And fast.

"But…but… I—I'm so afraid…. I don't like the thought of people sneaking around here doing… Why anybody… They could do anything. When I'm here alone…."

Phillip forgot all about the two sleazes in town. His only concern was for her. He had to call Wainwright and Cole Yardley, but that could wait.

"Nobody's going to hurt you," he said gently. "Nobody. Not ever. Because I won't let them. Understand?"

"But what if they come and you aren't here?"

"I'll be here from now on until this blows over. Juan can do most of the errands. I can write lists. He can shop. My credit's good in town."

"Oh, Phillip," she breathed, hugging him closer. "It's you I'm worried about. I called Ricky Mercado and he told me everything that happened in Mezcaya. He told me all about that man you killed and how his son is after you—"

"That bastard."

"Ricky—"

"Oh, so now it's Ricky—"

"He's your friend. He doesn't want you to die anymore than I do, and I don't want El Jefe's men to kill you. I couldn't live if anything happened to you."

"I feel the same way about you. That's what I've been trying to tell you. That's why I asked you to marry me." He waited until her racking sobs subsided and she stood still against him. "It's going to be okay. I swear I'll find out what's going on."

"And you're going to tell the sheriff. You're not going to act like you're so big and tough you won't call the law. You're going to tell him about the cows, about all three cows."

"I'll call him first thing. As soon as you're calm. Shh. Shh…" He stroked her back and her neck and then threaded his fingers into her hair.

When she quieted, he took her hand and led her inside the house. Then he picked up the phone.

"Sheriff…"

She sighed with obvious relief. But her fear didn't go away.

He called Yardley.

Her eyes grew huge when Phillip hung up and strapped on a gun. She followed him around even when he went out to the pastures.

That night he told her to dress up, that they were going out to dinner.

"What's the occasion?"

"No occasion. You'll feel braver somewhere else won't you?"

"Yes. Oh, yes."

Again he took her to dinner and dancing at the Lone Star Country Club. Again she dressed in her flashy red dress. Only tonight they ate in the club's formal dining room, which was decorated in blue and white, and they had a candlelit corner all to themselves. They held hands. They danced again and again, putting on quite a show for the other diners. When their first course arrived, they returned to their table and talked just like an old married couple who were easy and sure of one another, but beneath their conversation, the atmosphere between them sizzled with excitement. Not to mention fear.

After dessert, which was some sort of cream topped with luscious raspberries that melted in his mouth, he blew out their candles. He slid a hand in his suit pocket and laid a small velvet box in front of her. When she gasped, his big brown hand nudged it toward her.

"Open it, darling."

"Darling? I think I can guess what it is." Her voice

was so soft and wistful, he had to lean forward to hear her.

Gingerly she flipped the lid a couple of times before he grabbed it and opened it for her. An enormous solitaire sparkled against black velvet, and she cupped her mouth and cried, "Oh!"

"What's wrong?"

"It's huge. Too huge."

"I thought you liked flash. So, do you? Do you like it?" He took the sparkling gem out of the box and slid it onto her finger.

She flexed her hand. The gem shot fire.

"I—I can't believe this—" she began, fighting tears. "Nobody ever gave me…" Then she strangled on her words and the rest of her sentence was an incoherent jumble.

He looked at her, only at her, his heart pounding painfully against his ribs while he waited, his dread mushrooming when she lowered her eyes and couldn't seem to meet his gaze.

Her lips tightened. Then she began to bite them as if in confusion. Then very slowly she slid his ring off and gently laid it in his palm. Her fingers were shaking convulsively and tears were rolling down her white cheeks.

"Why not?" he rasped.

"I—I don't know, Phillip. It's too much…too soon. I mean…marriage…forever…you…me…Mission Creek… and children, too… Those cows…"

"We'll solve that mystery."

"But—"

"Where do you see this relationship going?" he demanded, changing the subject.

"I…I… Why can't we just be?"

"I'd like to be able to count on...our future. Wouldn't you?"

"You want to plot the rest of our lives all out like a war or something?"

"No. Not like a war. War is hell. What are you running from, Celeste?"

"Nothing. Nobody."

"Is it just me, then? Me that you don't really want?"

"Oh, Phillip, how can you even think such—"

"Or does it have something to do with the two guys that are asking questions about you? What do they have on you?"

"Two guys?" She pushed her chair back and would have raced away in a blind panic if he hadn't grabbed her wrist. "Who? What guys?"

"A couple of men have been asking about you in town. I would have mentioned them earlier, but we had to deal with the dead cow. Who are they?"

Again she struggled to push her chair back, but his grip on her wrist tightened. "Not so fast. There's something else I'm curious about."

"Let me go, Phillip."

With his other hand he pulled an envelope out of the inside of his jacket and read the Nashville address out loud. "There's a tape inside. You're sending stuff to a producer, Greg Furman, aren't you? Why couldn't you tell me?"

"Where did you get that?"

"You still want to be a star, don't you?"

"Oh? I—I left that in the truck, didn't I?" Her hands closed around the envelope, and she stared at him with those big, luminous eyes that undid him. "I love you, Phillip. You have to believe me."

"Then why can't we have a simple conversation? Why can't you confide in me?"

"I didn't think you'd understand."

"You don't give me a chance to."

"You're so big and tough. A Marine."

"A retired Marine, Celeste." He paused. "I'm a human being."

"Your life is precise and… Me, I—I feel…so torn. My life was a mess when I came here. Sending the tapes…"

"So there were more of them?"

"I write him letters, beg him to let me audition. I send him songs, too."

"I see. You can't wait to get out of here."

"No. My musical ability drives me. It's not totally rational. Sending those tapes was something I had to do. I didn't think you'd want me to."

"Life isn't always 'either or' you know."

"It has been for me."

"For me, too, then…because you think it is. When were you going to tell me about the tapes?"

"Oh…oh… I—I don't know. Oh, why does everything have to get so complicated? Why are you asking all these questions?"

"Were you just going to walk out on me again?"

"Phillip, I…"

"Don't say any more." He slid the ring and the little velvet box into his pocket. "You've said way more than enough."

"But—"

"Let's just go home and put this evening behind us."

"But we haven't settled anything—"

"That's up to you—"

He waited. Oh, God, how he hoped she'd say more.

When she didn't, he let go of her wrist, and she stood. He slid his hand to the back of her waist and escorted her out of the elegant blue-and-white room and then through the grand lobby lit with ornate chandeliers. Only when they were outside in the dark beneath a full moon and a starless sky and there was no one to see their livid pain, could they relax a little.

"What are we going to do?" she whispered later when he was driving them home in the truck.

"This is your game. We're playing by your rules. You tell me."

"But I can't. I don't know."

"Then neither the hell do I."

She asked him if he wanted her to leave the next morning and he said no.

Over the next few days Wainwright and Yardley made zero progress on their investigation. The two sleazes from Vegas didn't turn up, either. So, Phillip and Celeste drifted, and drifting was hard for Phillip who was a natural leader who wanted to command not only battles but his life, as well. All he wanted was for her to talk to him and to answer a few simple questions.

But she wasn't used to sharing confidences. Maybe she didn't believe that doing so could bring two people closer. Phillip didn't know, and he didn't ask her. They slept together, but his proposal and his questions had erected an invisible barrier, so sex wasn't as spontaneous or as hot as it had been before.

Now it was sweet and sad and desperate, and yet if it was all he could have of her, he'd settle for the crumbs he could get. He was that pathetic. They were drifting apart, and it was killing him. And there wasn't a damn thing he could do about it but hope that if he waited, somehow, some way, he'd get a break.

And then he did.

Only it wasn't the lucky break, he'd prayed for. It was a disaster that sent their lives spinning out of control in a horrible new direction.

Eight

Later that particular Saturday night after she'd driven off from the Saddlebag in his truck, and left him alone at the bar and he was drowning his sorrows in a bottle, in lots of bottles, all different kinds of bottles, Phillip would relearn one of life's dirtier little tricks. No matter how sudden the catastrophic blow falls, the aftermath is slow and deadly, the better to prolong the victim's agony.

Not that he had the slightest premonition of what was to come as he led Celeste up the steps of the plain-looking, wooden building that was the local bar. He simply felt edgy and unable to face another evening in the house alone watching television while she avoided him, content to read by herself in the kitchen while so many issues in their relationship were unresolved.

Didn't she care about him at all? Maybe she could float through life like a leaf going down a stream, but he needed roots. He needed answers, and he was nearly out of patience.

Feeling close to some dangerous, fatal edge, he shoved the door to the open bar and said in a grim, low tone, "Welcome to The Saddlebag."

As usual she was wearing lots of makeup and that flashy red number that didn't leave a lot to the imagination.

"You come here often?" she whispered, her voice a little shaky even though she was still trying to pretend that everything was all right between them.

"Before you came home I used to hang out here a lot. I shot pool, drank...dated.... And not nice church girls."

Celeste swallowed and wouldn't meet his eyes.

The inside of the bar was dark and cozy. A large bar ran along the far wall and there were about fifteen tables scattered in the middle of the room. In the rear, men were playing pool and shooting darts while their dates watched. A redhead in a tight black mini was yanking at the knob of the lone pinball machine and then pounding the machine and shouting when her balls didn't go where she wanted them to.

The walls were packed with Texas memorabilia. Maybe to avoid his gaze, Celeste was studying the old photographs of early ranchers, cow skulls, antlers, wagon wheels and branding irons with way more interest than they warranted. Somebody had filled a shelf with old beer bottles. She busied herself reading the labels.

Jake Hornung, a local cowboy, set down his pool cue and came over to them, studying her, too. "Long time, no see, Westin."

Westin tipped his Stetson. Nodding, he took Celeste by the elbow and kept walking.

"Nice dress. Real nice.... Hey, I know you." Hornung was practically drooling as he spoke to Celeste. "If you ain't Stella Lamour I ain't Jake Robert Hornung. A buddy said you sang at the Lone Star Country Club the other night, but I didn't believe him. Hey, I bought your album."

"You're the only man in America who did."

"How come you didn't do any more albums? I made copies for all my buddies. Hey," he shouted to his friends at the pool table. "Guys, Karla, this here is Stella Lamour, the country-western star."

A girl in a pink T-shirt that showed too much belly and tight jeans walked up to them and put her arm around Jake. "Stella... You're good, really good."

"I never met a star before," Hornung said. "Will you autograph—"

Celeste took a deep breath. She looked a little uncertain, but her admirers kept smiling at her and fawning over her every remark. Soon she became a little giddy and in the end when she had to sign about ten napkins, she couldn't seem to stop smiling.

A childhood memory came back to Phillip. One night his mother had put him to bed early and told him not to come out of his room because she was having a big party. Famous people were coming. She'd babbled off a few names.

When she'd turned off the light, he'd had a nightmare that he was falling out of an airplane and had awakened right before he'd hit the ground. Screaming for her, he'd run through the house.

She'd been out in the garden laughing with friends near thick banks of azaleas. As thin as a rail, she was exquisite in red, with a low neck that showed off too many glittering jewels. He'd yelled, "Mommy." Her smile had frozen. She'd nodded to his stepfather, who'd clamped a hand on his shoulder and ushered him back to his scary bedroom. His stepfather had been huge, and Phillip had been more terrified of him than of the demons hiding in his dark room.

"If you leave your room again, you know what will happen."

"I want Mommy."

"She's with important people."

"When will she ever want me?"

The next week they'd sent him to military school.

"Let's find a table, Celeste…or should I say Stella," Phillip muttered a little grumpily.

"Sorry about that," she murmured.

He led her away from the excited group, selecting a table as far from the pool tables and her fans as possible. A waitress came and he ordered them drinks and made up his mind to forget about the little incident.

"Sorry about that," Celeste repeated awkwardly.

Phillip was ashamed of his feelings and didn't know what to say. "Let's just get on with our evening."

"I know you don't like thinking about my music or my…career."

"Damn it. Is that what you call it—a career?"

Celeste looked startled. She was about to say something, and then choked back her words when the waitress brought their beers and placed them on tiny white napkins. He shoved a few bills on the table and ordered himself a second beer before he even started the first. "Long day," he said to the waitress.

"Cheers." He lifted his frosty bottle to Celeste and was aware of Hornung and his bunch at the pool tables watching Celeste and talking about her more excitedly than ever. He felt left out, so he drank deeply.

She didn't touch her drink.

"Are you ever going to tell me why you left Vegas?"

"Not now," she whispered.

"When, then?"

"Maybe when you tell me who's killing your live-stock. Okay?"

"Not okay. My livestock has nothing to do with you and me. Your secrets do. Okay?"

They sat at the table, not knowing what to say to each other. Hell, maybe she was listening to the band. Her fingers began to tap the table in time to the beat. Maybe she didn't need him at all. Maybe she just wanted her music. When he finished his second beer, he ordered two more. She frowned when he finished those.

"Don't worry," he muttered, tossing her the truck keys. "You can be the designated driver—*Stella.*"

"Stella? Why...why you're still sulking because I got a little attention."

"The hell I am."

"You hate my music, but it's part of me."

"I don't hate your music, but it led you into a dangerous life. You landed on my doorstep scared and broke, and you won't tell me why."

"Can't we discuss this when we get home?" she asked.

"Ha! You won't talk...except in bed. How long will we last if sex is the only thing holding us together?"

"Sex? You think that's all—" The devastation in her face cut him to the quick, but he wasn't about to let it show.

The band took a break.

"Stella. Stella. We want Stella."

Phillip turned just as Hornung got on the stage and told everybody that his favorite country-western star,

Stella Lamour, was here tonight, and if they were nice and clapped for her, maybe she would sing.

"Hell," Phillip whispered as everybody else began to clap and yell her name.

"Oh, God—" His brown hand curled into a fist.

"Take me home, Phillip."

"Hey, your music's everything to you. Who am I to stop the great star, Stella Lamour? Sing, Celeste, sing your heart out. You know that's what you really want to do."

"I want you, too."

"In bed maybe. But I wonder how much…and for how long? There's something you're keeping—"

She paled. "You keep things from me, too."

"To protect you, damn it."

"I don't want to quarrel like this…. Not with you."

Hornung got down on his knees and said please, pretty, pretty please into the mike.

"Maybe I will sing. It's better than quarreling."

"You're right," he whispered, ashamed suddenly. He didn't hate her music. He hated that she wouldn't level with him. Phillip stood and forced a smile as he helped Celeste out of her chair. "Break a leg—"

She took a deep breath and then, cocking her head to one side, Stella Lamour strutted up to the stage like the star he knew she wanted to be more than anything, more than she wanted him. She took the mike and paced nervously a moment or two.

"I wrote the song I'm about to sing for a very special guy."

Oh, God.

She turned toward Phillip, her gaze locking on his face. Did she have to be so exquisite in that red dress that was almost a carbon copy of the one his mother had worn the night she'd decided to send her little boy to military school?

Celeste shook her blond hair so that it caught the light and sparkled as it tumbled over her slim shoulders. She smiled at Hornung, at the rest of audience, at all the important people in the room. She was a born star. Suddenly Phillip realized that was one of the things that made her so special to him.

Only when she had the attention of every man in the room, did Stella turn back to him and begin to sing. Soon she was belting out her one and only country music hit, which, of course, Phillip knew by heart.

In the middle of her number, a man walked into the bar. Two more let themselves in a minute after he did. Not that anybody noticed them. Stella had everybody spellbound, especially Phillip.

Her blue eyes stared straight into Phillip's and he stared straight back. When she looked at him like that, with her heart in her eyes, he could barely breathe. She held him motionless in his chair until she was done.

"Nobody but you/Only you/And yet I had to say goodbye…"

Why, damn it? Tell me who you are and what you're so afraid of.

Only when she finished singing was he able to look away. Her music truly was a part of her. How strange, he thought that when she'd sung to him, he'd felt as connected to her as he did when they made love.

The other customers must have received a thrill or two themselves because they started clapping and stomping their boots and yelling for more. Hell, one song and she had the place in an uproar. The bar was charged with some new sensual power. Phillip remembered the first night he'd met her. She'd sung more than one song that night, and the place had gotten way too crazy. He'd fallen in love with her voice before he'd even known her.

Stella put the mike down and ran back to Phillip, her slim body carving its way through the excited throng as silently and gracefully as an elegant cat.

"Sorry about that," she whispered.

"No. You were great. Really great," he said.

"You really thought so?" Her big blue eyes seemed to burn his face.

Did his opinion matter so terribly? "Yes. I love to hear you sing. I always feel I'm the only one you're singing to. You were great!"

For an instant he thought he saw the spark of tears in her eyes, and he ached for the lonely little girl who'd grown up in foster homes. Gently he threaded his fingers through hers. Her smile was so radiant, his own heart nearly burst with happiness.

"Yes, you were great," said a hard voice behind them.

"Oh," Celeste gasped, caught off guard. "I didn't see you."

The stranger in the gray flannel suit was one of the newcomers. Phillip didn't know him, so he wasn't a local. The man tossed a business card onto the table. "Mind if I join you?"

Celeste picked up his card and flipped it nervously while she read. "Oh, dear! Greg... Greg Furman?"

The short bald man beamed, his teeth white, when he caught the shock of recognition in her voice. "The one and only."

"But you never once answered my letters— How'd you find me—"

"You put your address on every single envelope. I'm

closing a deal in Texas. So, I went out to your ranch, and this guy on a tractor said you were here. The last song you sent me was pretty good. Oh, it needs some work—''

''Pretty good? Oh, dear.'' She flicked a rapid glance up at him. ''Pretty good? You really think so—''

''Good enough for an audition in Nashville, Miss Lamour.''

''I—I can't believe...'' She turned to Philip. ''Oh, Phillip, this is wonderful. Just when I was about to give up forever...and settle....''

Settle? The word jarred Phillip's soul.

She looked past Phillip, but her dazzling smile faded when she focused on something or somebody behind him.

''Oh, dear....'' Her dying words were low-pitched and nearly inaudible. Phillip felt an icy prickle of danger. Something cold and deadly suddenly charged the air. Celeste went paper-white.

Furman was too full of himself to notice. ''Sorry, this has to be a short meeting, doll. So, look me up if you're ever in Nashville.''

When Furman got to his feet, he had to dodge a dark man and his paler companion, who were rapidly approaching their table.

The men sidestepped out of Furman's way and stared at Celeste with cold, flat eyes. Her lips quivered and she seemed to forget Furman and his exciting offer.

The two men were obviously some sort of threat. Her eyes grew huge when the dark man and his pale companion yanked chairs out and sat beside her without an invitation.

Phillip placed his hand over hers and pulled her closer.

He didn't need a formal introduction to know these were the two sleazes Mabel had warned him about.

"Please don't hate me forever," she pleaded under her breath to Phillip. The sadness in her eyes brought a bleak feeling of inevitability over him, too.

"Don't be ridiculous—" He broke off. "I couldn't ever—"

The band was still on break. The bar grew ominously quiet. Phillip's heart slammed against his chest.

"Whatever it is, it's time we face it…together," he said, tightening his hand over hers as the men stared at Celeste.

She licked her tongue over her dry lips and kept her wet lashes lowered.

"You two want something?" Phillip asked sharply. "I don't remember asking you to sit down."

"Yeah, we do…something from your lady friend…if you could call her a lady. You been hidin' out, using him to protect you?"

Celeste winced.

Using him? "Go to the ladies' room, Celeste," Phillip ordered in his Marine-issue drawl.

"They're my problem, not yours." Her guilt-stricken tone was jerky. Her hand was shaking in his.

"No arguments, Celeste."

She pushed back her chair.

"Hey, now, you ain't gonna run off from The Pope here, without giving him a little kiss for old times' sake?" jeered the pale reptile with the pimples and glasses.

"Go, Celeste!" Phillip's lips barely moved. "Now!"

"Hey, wait a minute, buster. We got business with Stella here." No sooner had the man with the pitted olive skin and big nose spoken than he lunged for Celeste.

Faster than lightning Phillip sprang between them.

"Whatever it is you're after, you're dealing with me from now on. Understand?"

Celeste swallowed a sharp, convulsive sob as Phillip pushed her away. "Go," he repeated.

"Phillip, please, please, please…let me stay and explain…." Her breathing was labored, and her beautiful blue eyes were luminous. "I didn't know how or where to begin before, but—"

He shook his head. "You're a little late."

She stared at him, as if to memorize his frozen features. "Oh, Phillip—"

The two men beside him began to fidget. They were getting restless. Celeste's eyes grew huge as she waited for them to tell Phillip about her.

Was it really so terrible? Why couldn't she have opened up to him before? If only she had trusted him enough to tell him whatever it was, dealing with these lowlifes would have been child's play.

But she hadn't. Just as she hadn't told him about her secret correspondence with Furman. His home had been a hiding place, a rest stop, a brief interval in a journey she'd intended to take alone to stardom.

Celeste's yellow hair gleamed. Why did she have to look like an angel even in her flashy red dress? She was very pale, scared to death and yet gorgeous. So gorgeous. A natural-born star.

Suddenly she seemed so far away…unreachable, like a star, heaven bound while he would always be an earthling. As he looked at her, he could feel his heart hardening, his body shutting down as it always did before a battle.

She seemed to sense the change in him, sense the total coldness. After a long time her breathing came under control and she raced toward the back of the bar.

Because of Celeste Phillip was about to cross a line he'd never crossed before. He was going to pay off these thugs or do whatever it took to get them off Celeste's back forever. He didn't care what she'd done, even if it was murder.

"How much?" he said angrily to the two men.

Nine

A hand with long black fingernails curled over the top of the metal door to Celeste's toilet stall. "Celeste, you in there?"

Celeste had put paper on the toilet seat and was sitting down with her shoulders hunched forward. Elbows in her red silk lap, her head was in her hands. When she didn't answer, the door jiggled.

"Go away," Celeste pleaded.

"Your big guy's right outside. He wants to talk to you somethin' awful. Says your friends from Vegas are gone and won't be back to bother you ever again."

"Not right now—"

A door banged open. "Man in the ladies' room!" Phillip shouted.

"Oh, my," the woman on the other side of Celeste's stall said. "Do you want me to call security?"

"No," Phillip said. "I want you to get the hell out of here."

"You're rude. That's my purse you're throwing...." The woman screamed and ran out the door after her purse.

A door lock clicked. Then a large brown hand jimmied her stall door.

"Celeste, damn it, do you think that flimsy door is really going to keep me out—"

She opened it. "I can explain—"

"Nero and your friend The Pope saved you the trouble."

"What..."

"Let's just say, I agreed to pay them a great deal of money. You're free to follow your big dream."

"But what if I don't want—"

"You came here to hide from those goons. True or false?"

"It's complicated."

"True or false?"

"True."

"You used me."

"No... I just wanted to hide. I needed a job."

"You seduced me so I'd protect you from them and pay them off so you'd be free to go on your merry little way."

"No..."

"Well, now you're free. Everything, the pretty smiles, the sex.... It's all been an act. Lies. You never wanted me. You wanted to be Stella Lamour, and you used me to make that happen."

"I love you."

"You knew they'd come."

"I didn't owe them anything. You shouldn't have paid…"

"They said they'd kill you if I didn't. They threatened me, too."

She blinked nervously. "They were after Johnny. He set them on me. I didn't tell you…because I couldn't bear for you to think badly of me. I didn't do any of those things they probably said I did. I'm not some—"

"I know exactly what you are—a woman I paid a great deal to sleep with. You let me use your body, but you gave me nothing else."

The room seemed to spin. His dark face was at the center of whirling white tiles and mirrors and fluorescent lights. Somebody was pounding on the door outside.

"Security!" a man shouted.

"Don't worry," Phillip said. "You were worth every penny. You've got Furman's card. And this, too." He pulled out a wad of cash and stuffed it into her red purse. "That's way more than you'll need to get to Nashville. Give your friend Johnny a call—"

"He's not my manager. He used their money to gamble and told them he gave it to me. Why won't you listen—"

"Maybe because you never trusted me enough to talk. Get the hell out of my life. A girl with your talents should go far."

"You said you loved me."

"Love." He laughed shortly. "There's no such thing. Not between us. You taught me that lesson—twice. We had sex. We used each other. You were scared and needed a soft landing. I was bored and needed a diversion in between wars. It was fun while it lasted, honey. But now it's goodbye. If we're smart, we won't pretend it was more than it was."

"You asked me to marry you."

"That's before I knew who and what you were. Why would I marry a shameless woman I've bought and paid for?"

"Shameless... How dare... Oh... You big, stupid lunk! You were a fool to pay them money I didn't even owe. You... I hate you. You're heartless.... You won't listen."

"Oh, so this is all my fault. I saved your life, and it's my fault?"

"You asked me why I wouldn't talk to you. Well, it was because I knew you wouldn't listen. You didn't before. You're arrogant and pigheaded. I knew you'd think the worst of me just like everybody else did when I was a kid. And you do. I just wanted a few more days with you...and a few more nights. I was that starved for love, that pitiful."

"Shut the hell up!"

"No wonder you're all alone in the middle of no-where—"

She flung open the door and raced past a short, fat man in a brown uniform.

"Miss—"

Phillip leaped after her, forgetting that she had the keys to his truck.

She was inside his truck and backing out before he caught up with her. Lunging at her door, he pounded on her window. She floored it, and roared out of the parking lot, her tires shooting gravel at him just like the chopper had in Mezcaya. All he could do was step back and cough in the dust. Another truck roared to life and raced out of the lot after her.

Hell. She was in no condition to drive. He stumbled

after the trucks. His booted toe hit a thick root in the drive, and he nearly fell.

Hell. He wasn't any more fit to drive than she.

"Celeste! Come back!"

His stomach went hollow when her red taillights disappeared into the gloom. Then the thick humid night wrapped him. Anything could happen to her out there.

"Damn it!"

He couldn't allow himself to feel protective or to worry about her. She didn't want him—period. Now that she was gone, now that he knew why she'd come and stayed, he felt gut-sick, rejected. He was alone. And there wasn't a damn thing he could do about it…except drink.

Tears clogged Celeste's throat and blurred her vision. She was driving so fast the truck was weaving from side to side, but she was too upset and irrational to think about slowing down.

So, Phillip thought she was low and cheap, did he? The weeks they'd lived together, all the lovemaking, everything they'd said to each other and shared, meant nothing to him. He believed every sordid word The Pope and Nero had told him.

She'd been right not to talk to him. Dead right. Well, at least she had her memories. She sniffed. They would have to hold her for a lifetime.

The straight black road was like an inky river under the stars through the wild, wide-open brush country. Why was she crying over a pigheaded hunk? She had what she wanted. She'd saved her paychecks, Phillip had paid off those devils and even given her more money. Furman wanted to cut an album.

Stardom had never seemed so close. So why were tears streaming down her cheeks?

High beams flared in her rearview mirror, blinding her. She'd noticed another truck had left the lot at the same time she had, but she hadn't really thought much about it. The driver flashed his brights and caught up to her. She slowed down and moved onto the shoulder so he could pass her.

Instead, he rear-ended her bumper so hard she could barely keep the truck on the road. Oh, dear! He hit her again. Whoever it was, was trying to flip her or hijack her.

She gasped. Nero and The Pope! They must've gone outside to wait for her. She should have known the money hadn't been enough. Then she remembered the dead cows and the threatening notes. Could these thugs be from Mezcaya? Whoever they were, they wanted to hurt her.

When she stomped down hard on the gas pedal, the goons behind her did the same.

Where could she go? Not back to the ranch. Not without Phillip there. No, somehow she had to find a wide place and turn around. She had to get back to The Saddlebag and Phillip.

Oh, Phillip. She loved him so much. Now she realized she'd been so afraid of losing his admiration she'd kept the bad things in her life to herself. But love had to be about sharing, even the bad things. This time she would explain, and she would make him tell her everything about Mezcaya. She wasn't going anywhere until she made him listen. She wasn't leaving him until she was sure he knew how much she loved him.

The truck rammed her again. Even as she struggled to hold on to the wheel, her truck veered off the road, bumping over rocks and cacti, thrashing through tall grasses.

Her heart was hammering when she fought to turn the wheel and get back on the road. No matter what happened, she had to make it back onto the highway, turn around and get back to Phillip. When she was on asphalt again, she risked a glance at the speedometer. She was doing more than ninety-five.

So were the devils behind her, flashing their lights.

Phillip… Just when she saw yellow signs that indicated a rest area up ahead where she might turn around, the truck hit her again so hard she skidded out of control.

The truck was flying straight at a tangled clump of oak trees.

"Oh, dear…"

She slammed her foot on the brake and screamed for Phillip, but the truck was like a roller-coaster car out of control.

The dense black trees with their spreading branches loomed like a wall in front of her. She screamed again right before she hit them. After that everything seemed all right.

She was back home in bed with Phillip. They were laughing and kissing, and he was caressing her hair and telling her he loved her.

He understood. He loved her.

Everything was all right.

She wasn't dying. She couldn't be.

She was going to cut an album in Nashville, and Phillip was beaming proudly, begging her to marry him. She had Phillip and her music. He was right. Life and love and woman's dreams weren't an "either or" proposition. She could have it all.

A young thug with a permanent tan and a cigarette dangling from his pretty mouth leaned close to her.

"Help me," she whispered. "Phillip…"

He laughed and began to scribble something on a piece of paper. His handsome face blurred. Then she heard voices in a foreign language.

The next time she opened her eyes, the pretty thug and his friends were gone.

Everything was all right.

Time ticked by slowly. Then a light shone in her face, blinding her. She tried to move and a hot pain stabbed her in the right thigh.

"Phillip—" Her voice cracked in agony.

"Don't try to move," Sheriff Wainwright warned gently. "We're gonna have to get the Jaws of Life and cut you out of there."

"Phillip… I want Phillip… I love Phillip." Her voice broke. Nothing mattered nearly so much as Phillip.

Ten

The beer bottles he'd lined up like soldiers on his table blurred. Phillip blinked but, in the dimly lit corner of The Saddlebag where he sat sprawled, that only made bottles bob like swimmers. He whirled around, grinning drunkenly as he held up two fingers, signaling to the bartender that he wanted a couple more.

The door opened and a tall, dark man stalked inside and looked around. Not that Phillip noticed Ricky Mercado at first. All his attention was focused on the bartender, who was scrubbing dirty glasses and seemed to be deliberately ignoring him. Even when Phillip heard his friend's heavy tread behind him, he paid no attention. Instead he picked up a bottle and began to beat his table like a drum. The maddening bartender looked up and scowled at him.

"It's about time," Phillip rumbled, swallowing a string of curse words.

"Enough, old buddy," came Ricky's deep voice behind him.

"Leave me the hell alone, Mercado."

With a charming smile Mercado pulled up a chair and sat.

"You deaf?"

"There's an old raccoon that hisses and spits at me every time I walk out my back door. He radiates more charm than you, old buddy."

"Did you come here to insult me—"

"I came here to warn you and Celeste. Wainwright and Yardley grilled me about Mezcaya all afternoon. They think I'm to blame for your dead cows. I did some checking, and I'm pretty sure that crazy thug, Xavier Gonzalez, is in the neighborhood gunning for you."

Oh, God. "How the hell would you know that unless—" Phillip began in a hard, ugly tone as he nastily swung around on Mercado. *Unless you had secret dealings with the arms dealers?* Even in his inebriated state, he wasn't ready to accuse Mercado.

Still, Mercado's voice got icy, too. "My source is very reliable. He knew all about the cows and the threatening notes— If the feds didn't know something, that A.T.F. agent, Cole Yardley, wouldn't be here trying to sniff out Gonzalez's little gun-smuggling ring. Yardley keeps showing up at my place, suggesting I'm involved with running guns to Mezcaya. No matter what I say, he won't believe I quit the family."

"Go away and leave me alone. I've got worse things to deal with than Xavier Gonzalez or your personal problems."

"Do you? If Xavier's hell-bent on murder?"

"Get out!"

"So where's Celeste?"

"Where's my damn beer?" Westin spun his chair around. "Bartender—"

"So she's gone. For good this time?"

"Get the hell out of my face," Phillip muttered between his gritted teeth. Then he slouched back against the wall.

When Mercado leaned forward to say something else, Phillip whipped out of his seat so fast, the chair fell over. The cozily lit room swirled. Phillip's gut wrenched queasily and he felt himself swaying. Mercado shot to his feet and grabbed his arm to steady him.

"I don't need your help. I don't need anybody's help." He bent and swiped at the beer bottles, laughing when they fell like bowling pins and rolled off the table.

The phone rang, and the bartender rushed up to them and said something fast to Mercado.

Pushing his friend, who suddenly looked dazed out of his way, Phillip stumbled toward the door, blearily amazed at how heavy his feet were and how damned hard it was to walk in a straight line.

Mercado caught up with him and lunged at the massive door beneath the exit sign, barring his way. He was holding a cordless phone against his broad chest with one hand.

"You're in no condition to drive." Mercado's expression was strange, scarily strange. His dark eyes held pity and compassion and something else—was it fear?

Mercado said something—maybe Phillip's name, but the words ran together in a jumble.

"Celeste," Mercado said in a low, shaken voice. Then he held out the cordless phone. "It's Wainwright, the sheriff.... They've made headway on their investigation. But there's been an accident. Celeste... They think Xavier or his thugs—"

"Celeste?" *Oh, God.*

Phillip took a sharp, painful breath and then he grabbed the phone. But he was so clumsy, he knocked it out of Mercado's hand onto the floor. Then he toppled to his knees, scrambling for it like a madman. By the time he picked it up, it was dead.

"She's in the Mission Creek Memorial Hospital," Mercado said.

"She's alive?"

"Somebody ran her off the road."

"Deliberately?"

Mercado nodded. "The bastards left another note. Celeste gave them a description of Xavier Gonzalez."

"Xavier?" *Oh, God.* He'd find Gonzalez and make him pay.

He shouldn't have been so rough on her. She'd been too upset to drive. If she died, it would be his fault—

"An ambulance took her to the hospital. That's all I know."

"She could be dead already."

Just the thought caused a blackness to close around his soul. He was a rejected little boy again with no place to call home.

What a bleak, dead place the world would be if anything happened to Celeste. He imagined her face still and white in a coffin. He had to get a grip, to shut down. Only he couldn't.

Terror that she was gone and it was too late for them wrenched him out of his self-indulgent abyss of idiotic self-torment into a totally different kind of hell, a hell that didn't allow him to shut down, a scary hell he had to face.

"I have to see her. I have to make sure they're taking

good care of her. You can't trust hospitals. Terrible things happen in hospitals. People die.''

''I'll drive you,'' Mercado said. ''But first, I'm getting a cup of coffee down you—''

''Just get me to the damn hospital.''

On the way over, all Phillip could think about was Celeste. Who'd hurt her? Xavier's men?

She'd been driving his truck. Xavier's men could have gone after her just because she'd been in his truck. He'd get to the bottom of this mystery, but first he had to make sure Celeste was okay.

If she wasn't all right, he'd die, too. Maybe not physically, but without her, his life would be flat and empty like before. Only worse.

He remembered the seven years after she'd left him. Seven years of fighting other men's wars. He hadn't cared whether he'd lived or died. When he'd been home rumbling around the empty ranch house without her, he'd seen her in every room. He'd tried dating other women, but nobody had ever come close to filling the void.

When he'd gotten home from the Middle East and found her gone, he'd been so hurt and furious that when she'd invited him to Vegas or offered to come back for a visit, all he'd said was, ''Follow your dream. You don't want me.''

What if she had? Maybe it was his fault she'd gotten into so much trouble. Maybe she could have found a way to be a singer and a wife. Maybe he should have supported her instead of demanding her on his terms. He thought of how she'd smiled when her fans had praised her tonight. Her music and the thrill of singing to an audience was part of her. Her voice thrilled him, too. It was why he'd fallen in love with her. She was a natural star. He'd been a selfish bastard to even try to take all that away from her the first time. He just hadn't realized back then how much her music mattered to her. And to him. To hold her, he had to give her her freedom.

As for Xavier... Phillip shouldn't have left Mezcaya with him alive.

He buried his face in his hands. The fear that gripped him was worse than anything he'd ever experienced in combat. He was helpless and scared, and his macho, tough guy act wasn't going to work this time. He couldn't shut down. The pain and the fear were inescapable. Never in his whole life had he felt so vulnerable and exposed.

"Celeste. Please, God, or whoever's listening up there... Please don't let her die."

"Phillip. I want Phillip...."

Celeste was in the hospital. Her broken leg was in a cast. Tubes were attached to her arms.

The door to her hospital room opened.

"Phillip..."

But it wasn't Phillip. It was a redheaded nurse with a syringe in her hand.

"I don't want a shot. I want..."

"You need your rest."

Even as she shook her head, Celeste felt the faintest prick in her arm and sweet fire tingling in her vein.

"Do you remember crashing your truck?"

She swallowed. "There's a weird taste in my mouth."

"Here, sip some water."

When she tried, she could barely lift her head or swallow. Within minutes her eyes felt heavy and her mind was drifting. "Phillip..." But Phillip wasn't coming. He didn't want her. He'd made that clear. She wasn't worthy.

Sick at heart, she shut her eyes.

Hours later she woke up and Phillip was there. Only this time she didn't believe he really was. It was a dream, like the one she'd had after the accident. Oh, the heartache when she realized her mind was playing another cruel trick.

"Go away," she whispered. "You don't really love me. You don't…" She shut her eyes, willing him to vanish.

"Celeste," he drawled in that velvet tone he used when they made love. "I'm sorry. I don't care what you did. I love you. You're the most wonderful thing that has ever happened to me. I love you."

"Hello," she said softly, opening her eyes.

He smiled.

"Hold my hand," she murmured. "Touch me so I'll know you're real."

He smoothed her hair out of her eyes. "I'm real."

"I'm okay," she said. "I have a broken leg. A minor fracture…"

"The doctor told me."

His hand stroked her cheek lovingly.

"Your truck's totaled, though. I—I was driving too fast when that other truck…"

"I don't care about my truck or even about who did this, just as long as you're…" His voice broke. He crumpled a piece of paper viciously in his hand.

"What's that you're holding?" she whispered.

"Just a note somebody left… Nothing."

"Did somebody kill another cow and leave you a note?"

"It's not important."

For a second or two her tough Marine stared past her out the window. He was too choked up to talk.

"Another warning?"

He pressed his lips together and nodded. "You're all that matters," he whispered. "You have to believe me."

She squeezed his hand. "So are you. I won't go to Nashville. I'll give it all up for you. I wanted to be somebody because I thought I was nothing. But you make me feel...special. Our life together, our future, is everything. I want children. Your children. Oh, Phillip, I was such a fool."

"You don't have to give anything up for me. You have a big dream and you tried to make it come true. You wouldn't be you without your dreams. I want to help you make them come true."

"You're my big dream. I just didn't know it. I was on a path. I had tunnel vision. You're everything."

"We'll work it out. Your music is a part of you. If fame and fortune ever threatens to overpower us, we'll deal with that, too. Together. If you want to sing, I want you to. We'll hire a housekeeper."

"Oh, Phillip I don't know. We'll have to see. Right now just knowing you love me is enough. But you'll let me sing if I feel I have to? You love me that much?"

He rained gentle kisses along her brow. "Now that I'm sure of you, I'm not intimidated by your music."

"Maybe I have a broken leg, but I feel so wonderful, so cherished. I—I didn't want to discuss my past life...because I was ashamed of it, or my dreams because I thought they threatened you."

"You don't have to explain anything. I was a jerk.... Pigheaded...I believe you said."

"No. You took me in when first came here with nothing even though I'd hurt you terribly."

"We hurt each other. You're a wonderful woman."

"I—I was so ashamed…when I got here. So ashamed of being such a miserable failure. I was afraid those guys might show up, and you'd think the worst."

"Which I did—"

"I—I wanted you to think well of me—"

"I do, in spite of how I acted tonight. Forgive me for that momentary lapse of sanity. I was jealous. It drove me crazy that you refused my ring and that you didn't trust me enough…"

"I do trust you. I was crazy not to before. Nobody's ever been so good to me before."

"That's all that matters." He cupped her face with his hands. "You made a mistake. You didn't do anything really wrong."

"Johnny gambled and didn't pay the money back he lost. When I gave him some money because he was desperate and I felt sorry for him, the goons after him came after me."

"No good deed goes unpunished." Grimly, Phillip thought of Xavier and what he'd nearly done to Celeste.

Phillip forced a hollow laugh. Then her eyes welled with unshed tears.

"Let's forget them…and concentrate on each other," Phillip said, leaning forward to kiss her as he stuffed Xavier's note into his pocket.

"What about the dead cows?"

"I'm almost certain a creep named Xavier Gonzalez from Mezcaya killed them and did this to you. He will pay. Apparently, he's got a nasty little operation running guns from Texas to Mezcaya, and he sees me as a personal threat to his business. Nobody knows where Gonzalez is right now, but I swear we'll catch him. So, your focus is to get well. Mine is to keep you safe."

She ran her hands through his hair and sighed.

"The mystery is all but solved. The bad guys will be brought to justice," he promised as he traced her cheek with a rough fingertip. "You have nothing to be afraid of. Nothing—"

"Nothing…to be afraid of…because I have you to protect me." She smiled at him with joy and love in her eyes. "I was right to come home to you." She felt completely happy, maybe for the first time in her life.

"Oh, Phillip, Phillip, my darling…. When I drove off from The Saddlebag I thought I wouldn't ever see you again, that you wouldn't want me. I was in hell."

"Me, too. I love you."

Tenderness at his velvet, reverent tone burst inside her like a new flower even before he put his arms around her and buried his face in her hair. Gently, without speaking, they held on to each other. Then he kissed her, a deep, long kiss that Celeste wished would go on forever.

Their souls and hearts were in that kiss.

"Forever," she whispered. "No more goodbyes. Only you."

"Forever."

He patted his pocket. "It's a good thing I held on to this big chunk of ice." He pulled out a familiar black velvet box and opened it.

"Oh, Phillip—" When she looked at it and then at him, her blue eyes flashed with more fire than his diamond.

"I've been carrying it around, waiting for the right moment."

"Looks like you found it."

He slipped it onto her finger. Bringing her hand to his

mouth, he kissed each fingertip. Not saying anything, he gazed into her eyes.

"Oh, Phillip—"

"Home. You've come home," he whispered. "To me, where you belong."

Epilogue

The long white limousine raced through gray storm clouds and thick driving rain toward the Lazy W. Dozens of cans tied to the back bumper rattled noisily behind them.

"Not very good planning...getting married during a hurricane," Celeste whispered as Phillip kissed her.

"Tropical depression," he corrected gently.

In the rear seat of the vehicle, the bride and groom soon forgot the cans and the rain or the damp satin streamers glued to the trunk of the car. They were kissing and holding each other so tightly, their bodies seemed glued together.

After another long kiss that left her breathless, Celeste held up her hand and gazed at her rings. All day, all during the reception, she hadn't been able to stop looking at them.

"Mrs. Phillip Westin," she murmured, glancing up at him. "Oh, darling, I can't believe you did it."

"We did it."

"I'm a respectable married woman."

"Don't let it go to your head. I mean, I don't want you to start acting…too respectable."

"You mean in bed?"

"Exactly."

She laughed. "I can't believe the whole town came to our wedding. Why, the reception at the Lone Star Country Club filled the club to its maximum capacity."

"And maybe then some." He grinned. "Free food and booze. It's going to cost us."

"I don't care. Everybody was so nice to me."

She still couldn't believe that the town accepted her because Phillip had chosen her to be his wife. They didn't care who she'd been before or if her wedding gown was low-cut and clung to every curve.

Now she was somebody, really somebody. Finally she had a family and a home…even a town to call home. She was loved and accepted. She was safe.

When the chauffeur pulled up to the big white house and got out and opened their door, Phillip wasted no time in getting her out of the rain. As soon as Celeste managed to get out of the car, he gathered her into his arms and carried her up the stairs and through the front door.

Inside, he let her go even though his eyes continued to hold her. Her knees felt weak because at last they were alone again. She knew what he wanted, what he'd wanted ever since the preacher had made them one.

Without speaking she reached up and began to undo the studs of his shirt. He slipped out of his tuxedo jacket as eagerly as if this was their first time. Soon she had the studs undone, and she'd managed to get him out of his shirt, too. He flung it on the floor impatiently, and she wrapped her hands around his lean waist.

His brown skin was hot. His eyes burned her.

"Oh, Phillip…"

"I can't wait," he said. "But then, I never can."

"Who says you have to? We're married."

"All those guests… I thought they'd dance forever."

"They're still dancing," she said. "We're the only ones who snuck out early."

"It's our honeymoon. We're entitled," he murmured, kissing her earlobe.

With awkward hands, he began to unfasten the tiny satin buttons at the back of her dress.

Then they were on the floor, and he covered her with his body. She closed her eyes and ran her hands over his thighs.

She felt something touch her abdomen, and she began to tingle all over. She giggled and grabbed at his hand blindly. "What…"

"Don't open your eyes," he whispered, "or I'll have to blindfold you."

Satin ribbons curled over her nipples, her eyelashes, and her throat. And then he touched her with something ice-cold.

"What's that?"

"Just be quiet. Enjoy."

"But it's kinky."

"Only the first time."

She knew Phillip deserved a proper, virginal bride. Not her. And yet he had told her over and over he wanted no one else.

She kept her eyes shut and surrendered to the sense of touch. For a long time different sensations played over her until she was quivery and nervy, and still he wouldn't take her. Then he licked her in sensitive places, and still with her eyes closed, she licked and touched him back.

He leaned over her. "Wrap me with your legs."

Instantly her legs came around him. When he drove inside her, thunder clashed outside and rain began to beat at the windows with gale force. The storm wasn't nearly as wild as she felt.

He said her name above the roar of the storm and she whispered his.

Never had she felt so hot or so desired. She was married. She belonged to him—utterly.

"I love you," he said. "I love you, Mrs. Phillip Westin."

Then he came, and she exploded, too.

"Being married just makes it better," she whispered a long time later.

"Every day, I'll love you more," he said.

"Oh, me, too. Me, too. You're my dream, my everything."

"Sing to me," he murmured.

"Nobody but you," she began. "Only you…" Her throat was suddenly too tight to sing.

"Don't ever say goodbye," he commanded.

"Everywhere I go, there's nobody in my heart…only you." She paused. "Enough singing."

"But not nearly enough loving—" He picked her up and carried her to bed.

"It's about time, cowboy," she purred when her golden head hit the pillow and he covered her with his much larger body.

She circled him with her arms.

He was all man, all hers, at last, forever.

*   *   *   *   *

Be on the lookout for
Ann Major's next book,
THE HOT LADIES MURDER CLUB.
It is due out in November, 2003
from MIRA BOOKS.
Please turn the page
for an exciting sneak preview...

One

Campbell never forgot a face. Never.

Joe Campbell's law offices with their sweeping views of the high bridge, port, and bay were posh. The tall ceilings, the starkly modern, ebony furniture, and the Oriental rugs reeked of money and power and social prestige—all of which were vital to a man like Campbell. Not that he was thinking about anything other than the exquisite woman he was supposed to be deposing. The case had been dull, routine, until she'd walked in.

She had him running around in circles like a hound dog that had lost a hot scent.

Her face was damnably familiar. Her husky voice was so exquisite and so raw, it tugged at Campbell on some deep, primal level.

He hated her for her easy power over him even as his cold lawyer's mind told him she was a fake. There was definitely something too deliberate and practiced about that lazy, luscious drawl. Nevertheless, she had him rigid with tension.

To distract himself he fiddled with his shirt cuffs. He'd asked dozens of questions and had gotten absolutely nowhere. She was a liar, and if it was the last thing he ever did, he would expose her.

"I—I swear I knew nothing, absolutely nothing about

any mo-o-old in the O'Connors' house,'' she repeated for at least the tenth time.

When he shot her his most engaging smile and leaned toward her as if the deposition were over, her lovely, long fingers and unpolished nails twisted in her lap so violently she almost dropped the damning photographs he'd jammed into her hands a few seconds earlier.

"I—I swear...no mold," she pleaded again.

Then why won't you look me in the eye?

"*Toxic* mo-o-o-ld." Campbell made his *o* last even longer than hers while his black gaze drilled her.

Not that she met his eyes or acknowledged in any way that he was mocking her. Instead, she shook her dark head like a true innocent and began frantically flipping through the photographs he'd made of the black muck growing inside the walls of the O'Connor mansion.

"There has to be a mistake," she whispered.

Her frightened tone made him feel like a total heel. Not that he let on how she affected him.

Campbell's long, lean form remained sprawled negligently behind his sleek, ebony desk. His beige silk suit was expensive. So was his vivid yellow tie. Hannah Smith, her knees together beneath her white skirt, sat on the edge of her leather chair opposite him. Flanking her was the attorney from her insurance company, a skinny, colorless little man. Hunkered low in his chair in that ill-fitting, undertaker's suit and those smudged, gold-rimmed glasses, Tom Davis looked about as dangerous as a terrified rabbit.

"No mistake," Campbell said. "The O'Connors have had to abandon their home. It'll cost more to remediate it than they paid for it, which was a substantial sum—"

"More than a mill— But it's not my fault!" she protested. "I was only the Realtor."

"Mold was not in your clients' disclosure statement."

"How many times do I have to tell you, *there was no mold?*" Her voice shaking, she began a boring repeat of her defense. "I can't be held liable for something I didn't know about."

"Maybe you didn't realize mold is a very serious issue on the Texas gulf coast."

"Don't talk down to me!"

He was supposed to be asking the questions. "And you are liable—"

She opened her pretty mouth, and like a fish out of water, gulped for a breath of air.

Hannah Smith was lying. And she wasn't all that damn good at it, either.

Joe Campbell, or rather just plain Campbell, as he was known to most people, at least to those with whom he was on speaking terms—and there were fewer and fewer of those in town since his line of work tended to alienate a lot of people—had been doing personal injury law too long not to be able to smell a liar a mile away.

Only she smelled warm and sweet. And thanks to his air-conditioning register that wafted her delectable fragrance Campbell's way, he was too aware of that fact.

Chanel. He frowned, shifting his long legs under his desk uneasily while still another unwelcome buzz of excitement rushed through him. By now he should have boxed her in. She was scared and pretty and he had her on the run.

And yet…somehow she had him off balance, too.

Nervously she shuffled the photographs of the O'Connors' estate like a deck of cards. Her slim graceful hands trembled so badly when she came to his damning shots of the mold, she nearly dropped the whole bunch.

"If they bother you, think how those images would affect a sympathetic jury, Mrs. Smith."

"That's not a question," her lawyer said. "You don't have to say anything."

Deliberately, she licked her lips with her pink tongue. "I'm sorry Mr. O'Connor's sick, but…"

Hell. She even *sounded* sorry. A jury would believe her, too. When she began talking faster and faster, swallowing, and glancing everywhere but at him, Campbell found himself studying her wide, glistening lips with way too much interest.

Sexy voice, intoxicating scent…and that delectable wet mouth…. Everything about her seemed soft and vulnerable. She was too damned likable. Very different from him. People who tolerated him said he was as hard as nails; they said he was ruthless, smart and cunning. His enemies said worse.

Campbell ran a tanned hand through his jet-black hair and sighed heavily. Then he yawned and pretended he was bored by what she was saying. Bored by her. If only he was, maybe then he could concentrate on the O'Connor case and finish her off.

She was tall, and she carried herself well. From the moment she'd glided into his office like an elegant gazelle on a runway, he'd been riveted by her exquisite lightness of being. Her catlike grace was almost professional, and yet something sweet and vulnerable screamed look-at-me, love me, please. Her every gesture, from her fluttery fingertips shuffling his pictures to her quick, nervous smiles at Tom—hell, even the pouty grimaces and frightened glances *he* got both charmed and maddened him.

A jury would be equally charmed.

Damn it, he had to get her….

LONE STAR COUNTRY CLUB
continues in Silhouette Desire...
Turn the page for a bonus look at
what's in store for you next month!
IN BED WITH THE ENEMY
By Kathie DeNosky
On Sale July 2003

One

"**H**aven't I had enough to deal with for one day?" Elise Campbell muttered when she missed the keyhole for the second time.

Waiting two hours for the judge to sign the court order had been a study in frustration. Then, having to listen to John Valente, the new head of the Mercado family, call her "doll" all afternoon made her feel like she needed a shower. Now, she couldn't see over the stack of files in her arms to fit the key into her door at the Mission Creek Inn. Thank goodness once she finally got inside, she could relax and be fairly certain that nothing more could go wrong.

Juggling her purse, the heavy stack of accounting records she'd just confiscated from Valente's office, and a small pepperoni pizza, she made another stab at fitting the key into the lock. In hindsight, she wished she'd made two trips from the rental car to her room, instead of trying to carry it all at one time. But with the mid-August temperature well over a hundred degrees, all she'd been able to think about was getting back inside to collapse in the cool comfort of the air-conditioning.

When she finally heard the quiet click of the lock's release, she quickly turned the knob, stumbled into the room, kicked the door shut behind her, and rushed over to dump everything on the desk. Shaking her arms to relieve the quivering in her strained muscles, she crossed the room to stand in front of the vent. The cool air blowing over her heated skin felt heavenly and she decided that after the day she'd had, she deserved a relaxing bath, then a glass of wine with her pizza before she started poring over the computer printouts.

Checking the connecting door between her room and the one next to it, she sighed heavily. The lock was broken. What else could go wrong?

When she checked in this morning, the innkeeper had given her the choice between the two rooms, so she knew the one next door was empty. But that didn't mean it would stay that way. Taking the chair from the desk, she jammed it under the doorknob. At least maybe it would slow someone down if they tried to enter her room without an invitation.

Twenty minutes later, she sat cross-legged in the middle of the queen-size bed, nibbling on a piece of pizza crust while she watched the six o'clock news. The weatherman promised that the rest of the month in south Texas was going to be a carbon copy of the past few days—hot. She glanced down at the shorts and tank top she'd pulled on after her bath. It was a shame she couldn't wear clothes like these to her job, instead of tailored suits and panty hose.

Shrugging, Elise reached for the glass of wine she'd

ordered from room service. She froze with the goblet halfway to her lips when she heard someone enter the room next to hers. Listening closely, she detected a single set of heavy footsteps crossing the room. Definitely a man. A dull thump followed by a succinct curse caused her eyes to widen. Either the man dropped a large piece of luggage, or a body. By the phrases he was using, she wasn't sure which. But whoever the guy was on the other side of the wall, he definitely was *not* a happy camper.

Moving her 9 mm Glock within easy reach, she slid it out of the holster and released the safety. She wasn't thrilled that the lock on the door connecting their rooms was broken, but there wasn't anything she could do about that now. She glanced at the chair still propped under the knob. If the guy in the next room really wanted into her room, a lock wouldn't prevent him from gaining entry any more than the chair would. Locks only slowed criminals down, they didn't keep them out.

When she heard the door on his side of the wall open, she gripped the gun in her right hand, extended her arm, then cupped the butt end with her left hand. She wasn't in the least bit surprised when the door on her side of the wall swung wide, shattering the chair as it crashed against the corner of the desk.

A very tall, extremely well-built man with short, dark brown hair and piercing hazel eyes stood like a tree rooted to the spot. "I want to know what the hell you think you're doing interfering in my case, Campbell?" he demanded, paying absolutely no attention to the gun pointed at the middle of his black T-shirt.

"And I want to know what you think you're doing barging into my room without so much as knocking, Yardley," Elise asked calmly, lowering the gun. She engaged the safety, then holstered the firearm. "Of course, that's the A.T.F.'s style, isn't it? Just storm in without the slightest thought about the consequences."

"No more than the FBI's style of sending a woman out in the field to do a man's job," he shot back.

Grinding her back teeth at the sexist barb, Elise refused to give him the satisfaction of knowing he'd touched a nerve. She smiled sweetly. "I see you haven't changed since the last time I saw you. You're still Caveman Cole, the A.T.F.'s very own knuckle-dragging Neanderthal."

He shrugged as he reached into the box on the desk to take a piece of pizza. "Some things don't change. Your tongue's still as sharp as ever." His hazel eyes twinkling, he gave her an amused grin. "But if you're wanting to know what my opinion is of female agents working in the field—"

"I already know all about them, Yardley," Elise interrupted as she unfolded her legs to sit on the side of the bed. "And I could care less. The fact that my superiors have confidence in my abilities is all that matters." Laughing, she added, "Your opinion certainly doesn't."

She watched a muscle jerk along his lean jaw. Her statement had irritated him. Good. She was pretty darned ticked off herself.

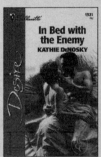

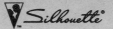

**Like a spent wave,
washing broken shells back to sea,
the clues to a long-ago death had been
caught in the undertow of time...**

Coming in
July 2003

Undertow

Cold cases were
Gray Hollowell's specialty,
and for a bored detective
on disability, turning over
clues from a twenty-seven-
year-old boating fatality
on exclusive Henry Island
was just the vacation he
needed. Edgar Henry had
paid him cash, given him

the keys to his cottage, told him what he knew about
his wife's death—then up and died. But it wasn't until
Edgar's vulnerable daughter, Mariah, showed up to
scatter Edgar's ashes that Gray felt the pull of her
innocent beauty—and the chill of this cold case.

Only from Silhouette Books!

Where love comes alive™